WHEN THE RAGING FIRE WEEPS

A NOVEL

SRIDEV MOHAN

To my dear World...

Contents

Contents

Foreword

When I was first asked to pen a foreword for *When the Raging Fire Weeps*, I was genuinely surprised because I didn't see that coming. I didn't know what to expect from the story either, and I prefer diving into stories like that. It only took me a few pages to get caught up in the intricate web Sridev had spun with this narrative. *When the Raging Fire Weeps* is set in the fictional Union Territory of Kolaazham, which also served as the backdrop for Sridev Mohan's earlier collection of short stories, *Life and Times in Kolaazham*. With this novel, he delves into the tumultuous world behind the making of an epic period TV show called *The Rhino Emperor*. It's a narrative where the drama off-screen is no less riveting than the spectacle on-screen, and I found that quite fascinating.

As someone who's always been as intrigued by the stories behind the camera as the ones unfolding in front of it, *When the Raging Fire Weeps* was a compelling read from the very beginning. Sridev captures the often sordid, sometimes glorious, but always intense realities of the fickle world of showbiz with a precision that makes the behind-the-scenes drama feel just as thrilling—if not more so—than the on-screen spectacle. The juxtaposition between real-life battles and reel-life performances is expertly done, and I couldn't help but appreciate the raw authenticity that seeps through every page.

As an artist myself, I understand the constant struggle with real-world circumstances to bring a vision to life, and *When the Raging Fire Weeps* echoes that truth in every chapter. The battles waged behind the scenes—the compromises, the challenges, and the occasional moments of triumph—are experiences that every creator, in some way, can relate to. In this story, Sridev not only captures those struggles but does so in a way that feels visceral and real.

With the rise of OTT platforms, the stakes in entertainment are higher than ever, and the demand for compelling content is relentless. What happens behind the curtain is now as relevant to the conversation as what's on the screen, and *When the Raging Fire Weeps* gives us a front-row seat to that chaotic, all-consuming process.

I hope Kolaazham continues to give birth to many more stories like this, and I wish Sridev Mohan all the very best with this novel and his future endeavors. It's a journey worth taking, and I'm sure readers will find themselves just as captivated as I was.

- **Rohit Ramachandran, ACS**
Author of: Baptism by Blood, The Gravedigger of
Qadim and Escape for Love.

Underneath all the sheen

If creating art was that easy, you would meet an artist at every crossroad and every corner and every day when you looked at the mirror. Anything created without much forethought and struggle, anything crude and underdone, would be considered art. The world would slowly fill up with mediocrity and slowly art would lose its meaning. If creating art was that easy, you wouldn't be reading this novel by Sridev Mohan. Art does not happen without hardships, without struggles.

If you dont know already, the author is an aspiring filmmaker. No wonder, the novel is set in the supposedly glitz and glamour world of cinema. The inner workings of how a scene conceived in one mind, translated into words and dialogues, enriched with scenery by the crew, enacted by the cast and shot with the best point of view it deserves - is all in the details here. But that is just a vehicle, rather a framework, to show us what goes behind those works of art you have seen umpteen times on the silver screen or the otherwise black mirrors of your smartphones.

Are you that person who quickly scans through the names when the credits roll after your favourite soap is over or are you the kind who would wait for that 'Skip To Next Episode' appear? Ever wondered what those names meant? How those people collaborated to bring you those perfect frames and in that process how their lives intertwined? The friendships, the conflicts, those bonds, those betrayals...

Yes I did say 'the supposedly glitz and glamour world', didn't I? I think it will not be fair if we don't mention the elephant in the room considering the recent happenings in tinsel town, happenings that sadly keep recurring. Underneath all the sheen and fanfare, the ugly teeth of the filmworld grins bare at us, albeit a few rotten apples. Some may say that this is not a first. This has happened before. But the courage to speak out - well, that's new. In that regard, it is my humble view that this novel will resonate with the conscience of the present.

- **Krishnakumar M, IT Professional**
Author of: Prethachandran, Davidinte Irippidam,
Duswapnam Pookkunna Maram

Preface

When the initial thoughts about bringing out some of my writings I had scribbled up over the years formed within, a new found excitement took hold of me. There were a few spec screenplays, an epic poem and few shorter ones and some short stories happening in a fictional union territory that were ready to transform into physical books. I could finally get to hold my writings in book form and share them with the readers around the globe. And thus my foray into publishing my writings finally happened with the short story collection Life and Times in Kolaazham Part 1 in 2021. I expanded my poetry collection, rewrote my screenplays and ruminated on more stories set in Kolaazham. I urge the reader not to consider these lines as boasting. No. The point here is the literature category that never figured in my creative space or endeavour was the format of the novel. Having been self trained (which is ongoing) in the art of writing screenplays, my mind always looked at characters and their settings rather cinematically, though how I wrote my short stories is still under speculation. I love to see the camera move forward or pan around or rise above or lower itself to tell a story. And so the novel writing idea took a back seat, way way back...

Time went by. And then a friend of mine, Rishikesh Bhat, added me to a group of readers and budding writers in Whatsapp, one fine morning. That was a total surprise. Though a teacher of English literature, I was not inclined enough to discuss writings of authors then. But then slowly the group took me in. And I bought some of the books of the budding writers including Arshad's, KrishnaKumar's and Rohith's. Arshad's was a short story collection, brilliantly written. There was a human touch to those writings. And then almost back to back I read KK's Malayalam novel Prethachandran and Rohith's English novel The Gravedigger of Qadim. Apart from the captivating stories the books discussed, it was the zeal in the writings that shook me more. A type that maybe missing in the works of established writers. That shifted the dormant literary gears of the dusty sidetracked novel writing projects that I never found interesting. As an aside, I did attempt a story in the novel format once. One line later, I dropped the idea.

But this time it was for real. And the real push came when I was watching the massive series The Vikings that cemented my burgeoning desire to write a novel, a novel about a tyrant king and his heartless exploits. Only the king and I were there initially. But as we began discussing the project, more characters joined in. From August 18th till 30th '24, I had one of the most thrilling creative spurts ever. No writer's block, no confusion, no creative fatigue... The first draft of 'When the raging fire weeps' thus came to life, my debut novel. I strongly believe that if the story and the writer is in sync, the characters in that story will take the writer along. A smooth ride is guaranteed. And in time, the creative power within will find a way. Despite having read several novels, short stories and poems, those works never inspired me to write a novel. But two budding writers did - KK and Rohith. I am thankful to Rishikesh for adding me to the group, Anup for our brief discussions about mythology, Arshad for his short story Oreo and the king, Arya for introducing the enigmatic poems of Satchidanandan to me. All these peoples' literary interests have somehow found a place in my first novel. I also thank all the members of the Literature and More Whatsapp group for instilling in me a different kind of love for literature. My creativity has much to do with a clear-cut mind that gets assistance from my loving wife who is there, ready with inputs and support. In early 2024 when we entered parenthood, our son assisted us in getting into that new role. Even though it may sound crass, I still wish to thank our baby son in letting us know the excitements related with raising children, but most of all gifting us the great cosmic spiritual journey called parenthood.

My sincere thanks to Dr Parvathy Anoop for giving her invaluable thoughts about this work, especially from a literary standpoint. My sincere thanks to KK and Rohith for their meticulous observations and constant support. My sincere thanks to my parents for instilling in me the love for literature in my early years. My sincere thanks to friends and foes. My sincere thanks to fate. My sincere thanks to Notion Press. My sincere thanks to creativity. My sincere thanks to my beloved Kolaazham. Let me finish by reminding the reader that this is a fictional work. I have no intention of hurting any job, person or religion through this novel.

Sridev Mohan
   30/09/2024

Prologue

In the Norse Mythology, the handsome god of truth and light, Baldur, had begun to have nightmares about his death. His mother Frigg, wife of Odin, took a journey across all the worlds and sought assurances from all the plants, animals, metals, forces of nature, diseases and all of existence etc that they wouldn't harm her son. Frigg didn't consider asking the insignificant mistletoe's assurance though. Loki the trickster god found out about that loophole. He made the god of darkness, Hod the blind brother of Baldur, throw a mistletoe at him. Baldur died on the spot. The sudden death made the worlds fall into irreparable grief. There was despair across the realms. Every part and parcel of the entire gigantic creation *wept...*

CHAPTER I

The Rhino Emperor

The Rhino Emperor emerged from the makeshift bath glad like a baby, the wobbly bulging stomach a disgust to watch. On that hot summer morning the first sounding of the horn alerted the drinking soldiers to file into two long lines that stretched to the horizon. In the king's tent, an ever-jubilant Jeyopola with his huge bulging stomach was squeezing and kissing some semi-naked young women who were in the midst of dressing him in royal attire. In the queen's tent, Margafa too got dressed, her face showing no signs of excitement. Soon the second horn sounded. King Jeyopola mounted the tenth elephant among a hundred, fitted with a palanquin decorated with a royal panache. On his lap sat his beloved mistress, the semi naked Himsha, the dark-skinned seductress. With the third sounding of the horn, the long line of soldiers, horses, elephants and the royal entourage started to march forward. The thumping sound of that massive group was thunderous. The dust rising from the ground resembled a desert storm. As they crossed the walled city, a dejected mass of local people looked on with gaping eyes as they witnessed a thousand, no, an innumerable number of horses and men marching through the fallen kingdom's massive iron gates. Following the horses were the foot soldiers somewhere near to three thousand, all muddied and bloodied, but with victory written on their foreheads. Then entered the hundred elephants. Several dejected eyes felt mesmerised seeing that sensuous woman with the old king among all those gory, dusty men. As for Jeyopola, even while caressing

Himsha, he was greedily scanning the street for young female bodies. Many women hid behind pillars, behind their fellow men, behind anything possible to avoid that dirty man's covetous gaze.

Tied to one of the hind legs of the tenth elephant was the badly wounded king Walika of the defeated kingdom. The dejected people cried having to see their erstwhile king be treated this way. Soon the cavalcade stopped. Walika was signalled to be untied as the elephant upon which Jeyopola sat lowered itself for the old man to press his feet upon his new addition to his huge empire. The injured Walika was made to stand close to the victorious Jeyopola who warmly embraced Walika and pointed to a tree not far away, with a genuine smile. Walika looked towards that point. His feet gave way and he fell to the ground wailing like a madman. It was then that the townsfolk too noticed that ghastly sight. One old woman let out a cry saying, 'The king's children...'. How swiftly had Jeyopola's men hanged the three young children of Walika no one could fathom. But, there, on that tree branch was dangling the corpses of three children gently dancing with the breeze as the ropes creaked.

Jeyopola now ordered his men to drag the fallen king into the royal hall. The royal hall was something Jeyopola never could have imagined. Ruby studded walls, massive red pillars, an air-cooling system of some kind inside the hall, some sort of fragrance filling the air... This was heaven indeed. And then as though struck by a lightning bolt Jeyopola stood motionless. The entire body of people behind Jeyopola stood just like he did. Then, the mistress Himsha came forward and hissed into the old king's ears, 'I am yours, so is that throne. Go and devour it, my king.' Out of the blue, Jeyopola got hold of Himsha's hair which pained her, though she didn't show it. Jeyopola threw her to the ground and raising his feet to stomp her he yelled like a monster, 'You whore!! How dare you teach me what to do!!'. He was about to kick her but then he felt the throne beckoning him. Jeyopola walked towards the throne as though in a trance. Himsha raised herself up, bruised, insulted, but she had to carry on. She tried her best to walk, shaking her body seductively, which was actually shaking from fear.

The aging king now sat on his grandfather's aging throne for the first time. There was dust and sweat rolling down the fatty figure of the old man as he sighed a hearty relief, once he placed his buttocks onto the throne. He spread his boulder size thighs and slapped his thighs indicating Himsha to sit on one. The young woman feigned lustiness, walked up to the throne and sat on her master's thigh. Jeyopola then kissed Himsha. There was a 'sorry' in his eyes and a 'don't talk to me' in Himsha's. Just then, Jeyopola let out a thumping fart. The ripping sound emanating from the victor's bottom reverberated across the royal hall, onto the town square and into the hearts of the public beckoning a horrific fear coming alive. Following the 'fart of the millennium where even the gods took shelter', as the newly appointed poet of the court jotted down, king Jeyopola of Surnamia took the reins of his long-cherished sea faring enemy land, king Walika's Chaapikia, under his control.

Now, it was time for Jeyopola to cry. He cried like no man of immense power had cried before. He cried as though it was his last day on earth. He cried as if *he* was the prisoner of war. Jeyopola cried because he had done what his father and grandfather could not do. The eighty-year-old had amassed great energy – through sacrifices of animals and people – and the gods were once and for all truly happy to grant Jeyopola's rightful throne back to him, to his clan.

Before deciding on what to do with the prisoners, Jeyopola decided to destroy Walika's wife, the queen Yalaya's honour. The young queen was dragged to the center of the hall, and as everyone looked on, Jeyopola now undressed himself, walked towards the queen while his soldiers stripped off Yalaya's clothes and made his lusty body slither through hers. She tried to remain calm, even as immense tears of pain trickled down her cheeks. Her husband had had the bad luck of having to see this brutal act as his eyelids were forced open with an apparatus. Walika screamed. Yalaya remained silent. Jeyopola moaned like a wild beast. For a second, even Jeyopola's soldiers felt if their king did this act in a closed room. Himsha stood near the throne, with a lump in her throat.

Walika's children were lucky to not have seen this scene as they had been ordered to be hanged once Walika had acceded to defeat. The defiling of Yalaya was now complete. Jeyopola got up and ordered his men to have their share of the queen. Many soldiers happily dragged her away. The red eyed Walika now screamed, 'Death shall befall you like none known to humanity, you old bastard!!'. Walika screamed once again and spat out blood as he got a knock on his nose by Jeyopola's soldier. The next blow came even harder. This time it was Jeyopola himself. And as Walika went flying into the air, and onto the floor with a thud, he was actually amazed at how surprisingly strong the old Jeyopola was. Walika's head hit the floor. His skull cracked. He died.

Jeyopola remarked, 'Make his army general clean the floor... with his tongue'. And the new king now exited the royal hall and made his way to the royal wash room, to have a bath. He ordered four of his Persian mistresses to join him. The women giggled and went after their master most obediently. The semi naked Himsha stood near the throne not knowing what she had to do. Just then king Jeyopola's queen, Margafa, entered the hall. With jealousy burning in her eyes, the middle aged Margafa looked at the young Himsha who reciprocated the look by sitting on the throne leg upon leg, with a sinister smile. As the new king left the hall, a female voice announced gently, "And there we call a cut. Scene One ends." She kept her pen down and continued, "Now, we had finished shooting the war sequence between Jeyopola and Walika along with the ending of season one four months back. Now we need to focus on the execution of this crucial ending scene, which I am planning as a single long duration shot. It is here that Jeyopola actually begins to turn into the tyrant, the trait that he carries on till the end of the new season."

The studio executives of Little Further Up were really impressed with Jaseela's confident narration of The Rhino Emperor's upcoming second season's first episode's massive ending scene. One executive enquired if the editing of the war scene had finished? It was still in the process was the answer. Little Further Up's studio facility in the Kolaazham Film Development Corporation's film campus was where the first season was shot. The upcoming season too was to be shot there, but with the sets of the series up for a major revamp.

Throughout the entire narration, Jaseela could see something was troubling Jonathan, the owner and CEO of Little Further Up. He didn't even bother to give her a lift to the airport after the narration and luncheon, which he usually did. Jaseela sat at the Dubai International Airport tensed. What was troubling Jonathan? Despite that tension,

The Rhino Emperor was filling her mindscape. She was afraid. She was excited more. Super excited. She took out her phone and decided to video call... her special man.

CHAPTER II

Action!!

Sprawling over an area of 260 acres, the mammoth sets of The Rhino Emperor's second season's various palaces, cities, oceans, arenas etc were meticulously built over a period of almost seven months even between the shooting of the first season. The first season required only around 100 acres; the story was beginning to grow. The second season demanded more space, more than double to be precise. The production design team spend a lot of time with Jaseela in finalising the sets. The most daunting task was creating an artificial lake in the set. In the story, that lake was actually a part of the sea. Jeyopola was attacking a sea facing kingdom. 3 million gallons of water had to be pumped in. Boats were made to row in the lake as a trial which was to continue as an attraction even after the series would stop after season three. The royal hall where Jeyopola sits on the throne was about 70ft in height and 150 ft in diameter and was built on an acre of land. The hall had to have massive pillars, massive windows, a mirror like floor, almost 300 seats etc. The defeated kingdom Chaapikia was thus literally bone breaking to build.

On to this man-made marvel, the very first dim golden rays flew to in advance and the following rays started to flicker from behind the Western Ghats, notifying the coming of the sun and with it a beautiful morning. Several rays dropped onto the lake providing an ethereal look to the set from a distance. The weather forecast for the day was predicted to be good. It was a good day for the massive trial shoot of the ending scene of S02E01. Around 100 vehicles had already plyed into the parking lot of the Kolaazham Film Development Corporation at 4:00 AM as a staggering 500 extras were brought in. All the extras were in awe as they entered the sets of Chaapikia. Of the 500, 200 or so would become the citizens of king Walika's defeated kingdom. The rest were to transform into the gigantic army of the victor, king Jeyopola.

The costume department had to divide their hall into two sections: the citizens and the army. The extras were given detailed instructions in advance as what to do and not to do in the sets of The Rhino Emperor. No mobile phones were allowed once inside the set. The extras had to don their respective attires, wear the required make up, have breakfast at the huge food hall readied, take a dump or pee if necessary and be at their assigned posts by 6:10 AM. The trial shoot would commence at sharp 6:30 AM. The dressing up and make up began at 4:30 AM.

The departments of costumes, make up and stunt were on their toes. The camera and sound departments were getting ready to stand and then run, on their toes. The canteen had begun preparing the food items last night itself, mostly vegetarian, to avoid stomach problems. A huge crowd with upset stomachs had only one possible outcome - disaster.

The team, under the able hands of Jaseela wanted to get a real feel of what it would be like to shoot that gigantic scene. Thus it was decided to make this trial shoot just like if they were going for a take. In the director's hut, Jaseela had finished her bathing and was sipping a black coffee. Jaseela was on the second day of her period. The trial shoot's hectic pressure was not enough, the biological side too had to pitch in. She was in great stress but that was not the time to show it outside. It was 5:10. Jaseela didn't sleep last night. The period. And all those doubts... Whom could she trust? That troubled face of Jonathan during the reading session in Dubai, almost six months ago, was still lingering in Jaseela's mind. She had doubts. The Rhino Emperor will be sabotaged. And most of all, *him walking out...*

Jaseela pushed her doubts, body pain and her lover's sudden desertion away as the major crew members came into her hut and they all joined together to do a last-minute brush up of the trial shoot of the massive ending scene. Jaseela was about to direct 500 people all at once. She let that thought seep in. After the brush-up with the crew, Jaseela moved to the royal hall where the main actors were placed. The actor playing the titular role began barraging Jaseela with several severe statements. He was so angry; Jaseela was completely taken aback. She was aware of the issues in his family. But Jaseela had bigger issues to deal with. She was already feeling lonely, now that the person whom she loved the most in this world, had walked out of the set, due to her doubts about the lover's sincerity.

Jaseela was beginning to crumble. But an intervention from some of the cast cleared the lead actor's grievances. He was so heaped with remorse; he literally fell at Jaseela's feet for forgiveness. Some of the crew and cast knew about who was trying to ruin the project. Anyway, who was Jaseela to forgive? She was no god. *She* needed forgiveness. The person whom she needed now, at this critical day, was not there with her. Jaseela needed that person's forgiveness... Somehow, Jaseela mustered enough strength to move ahead. 500 extras and about 170 cast and crew were waiting for Jaseela. She had work to do.

The brush-up with the actors went well. It was 6:00 AM now. Jaseela wanted to pass wind. But she withheld the tendency. She exited the royal hall. The final arrangements were done by 6:10 AM. Everyone was prompt. There was no confusion on anyone's part. Jaseela reached the spot. Once the trial shoot began, Jaseela would be everywhere in the set. She was meticulous. At 6:30 AM as she wielded the megaphone and shouted 'Action', there was no energy. That typical defiant tone was lacking in spirit. "Where are you, my love?"... Jaseela wanted that support badly. The writer/director of one of the biggest television series to ever grace the Indian screens, had faltered her voice once. It wouldn't happen again... No, she had to gather herself together; now was the time to pick herself up. Jaseela took a deep breath and then through the megaphone she screamed...

CHAPTER III

Jaseela

"Amma, I am leaving. The food is ready, kept on the table. I'll be back by evening. Ask Rukmini to clean the balcony today ok", said Jaseela as she closed the entrance door and started walking down the stairs. Her mind was filled with the first discussion session of the second season going to take place with the crew in the coming days. Something that Jaseela had been waiting for, for a long time. She entered the car park. She unlocked her car's doors, entered the driver seat. A sudden burp disrupted her train of thoughts. "The smell is good. I should have packed some semolina upma for lunch as well", thought Jaseela as she switched on her car.

The signal turned red. Jaseela was right at the front. Among the pedestrians who crossed her car, few actually noticed the celebrity writer/director behind the wheels. A college going girl saw Jaseela and waved her happy hands frantically. Perks of being the writer/director of one of the most successful shows to grace the Indian television, this lady from the Union Territory Kolaazham had made headlines when it was announced that the international media giant Little Further Up was planning to foray into Indian television, that too with an epic saga to be helmed by Jaseela Akbar, who now pressed the accelerator gently as the signal turned green.

Jonathan Meg, CEO of Little Further Up, had held several meetings with Jaseela in Dubai and London before coming to a multi-crore deal to produce what was now rocking the Indian television, The Rhino Emperor. The first season with a total of 6 episodes each running for an hour was a smash hit. There was treachery, bloodshed, sex, love, action and all that was necessary for an Indian epic. The Rhino Emperor was India's answer to the world. For the second season, Jaseela would get a whopping Rs 8 Cr as salary and additional revenue if the episodes did beyond what the makers believed would work. And she had a fling for Jonathan, which was generously reciprocated. Jaseela had had the pleasure of sharing her bed with a few Indian men. But a man from the west was the first. And boy was it a joy ride.

The first sleep they had together was when Jaseela had sat down to pen her first episode's screenplay for the first season in London. That physical union, that session, was so electrifying, that Jaseela wrote the entire one-hour screenplay, with a total of 157 pages, in just one day's time. Straight!! Literally no breaks in-between. A total of six electrifying, venomous, vivid, colourful sessions took place. Now, she was going to start writing season two's first episode's ending scene. But there was a difference. This time it was in Mumbai, one of her favourite cities. Jonathan had flown down to Mumbai to be with her. Jonathan had a family back in the UK. But that marriage was failing. And though Jonathan was around 15 years older to Jaseela, their bodies connected well and their minds were in unison, a perfect sync they never felt with anyone else before. So thought Jaseela temporarily.

The director and the producer made heavenly love. The rain outside added to the romance. The romance started turning wild. It was then that Jaseela had an epiphany. Yes!! The ending of the first episode of the second season had to be equally wild. No compromise. The protagonist had to be turned into a tyrant now. As Jonathan slept after the rocking session in the five-star suite of the Mumbai Equator Hotel, Jaseela sat on the bamboo chair, naked and caressing her long hair. She was thinking. She opened her notepad and began writing. Sometimes she would see the tyrant Rhino Emperor in Jonathan. Or maybe she herself was the Rhino Emperor. Or was it her ex-husband, that alcoholic maniac Nishad who burned her thigh when they came to know it was he who couldn't give Jaseela a child...

Jaseela Akbar had always dreamt of becoming a film director. Her father Akbar was the main man in Nirmesh Shetty Production Company's catering unit, where Akbar and his ten-member team had the responsibility of feeding the stomachs of the film star makers and film stars. Her mother, Jaan, was one among the team who worked from 4 AM in the morning till 8 PM in the night. This job which her parents did, lasted for about 36 years. Jaseela was now 35 and divorced. God didn't gift her a child. But she would often immerse in a debate with herself what it would be like to nurture a child single handedly. To be a single parent.

Jaseela and her twin sister Jameela had their parents' care despite the rush in the film catering unit. Both Jaan and Akbar made it a point to be there for their young ones when needed – from PTA meetings to buying dresses for Eid, from buying uniforms at the start of the academic year to being in the audience to cheer the children when they took part in their school's cultural events. Education was of utmost importance, something which Jaseela's parents couldn't receive in their younger days. Something which would be given to their daughters at any cost. As the years flew by, Jameela got married and flew off to Canada with her businessman husband. Theirs was a happy family. Shoukath was a good man. Though ambitious, he was a lot like Akbar, always there when needed. And so, Jameela gladly gave Shoukath three children. Three healthy children. Whenever Jaseela felt the pangs of her lost motherhood, she would fly to Canada, spend a few days with the children, all expenses paid by her, and she would return. It was not that she couldn't conceive, but that she was afraid. Afraid of the partner who may not be with her to take care of her child. Why push a child into unwanted misery? Jaseela ate and swallowed that pain silently. Maybe, just maybe, Jonathan might give her a child. Maybe three children.

Not knowing that life and fiction were merging, one of her characters, a defeated king's three children were seen hanging. The parent within that king screamed in pain. Despite not having gone through the painful process of delivering a child, tears rolled down Jaseela's cheeks. She wanted a child. She would propose to Jonathan. It would be a single static medium shot. Jonathan would rise from his sleep. He would see Jaseela who was outside the frame, but who would now enter the frame and come near the bed. She would lower herself to Jonathan and place his head on her bosoms. There, at that moment of deep care and protection, she would propose. Jonathan would accept. They would make love again while Jonathan would transfer a child into her body... Jaseela just then felt what she had been hunting for a long time. She *was seriously* in love. No, not with Jonathan. But with... She wanted to be with that man. With that man, she was *free*. Absolutely...

A romantic smile emerged on Jaseela's lips as she raised her hands to the air. And then she felt a stench coming from her armpits. The sweat from the 7th and final rocky session with Jonathan, in the bed, had turned sticky. Jaseela needed a bath. And so, she made the tyrant go for a bath with his mistresses while she decided to clean herself as well.

CHAPTER IV

Bhagath

The damage was complete when Bhagath's sister was born. To keep the explosive young Bhagath at bay, his parents would always pamper him and leave his young sister behind. He loved his sister so much. She only hated him more. Bhavathi had vivid memories of her parents showering love on her brother not because she was a girl, but because their elder child, her brother Bhagath was simply an angry spoilt brat. Bhagath still got pampered by his mother. That thought simply crushed his bones and soul. Oh that hellish cringe feel...

The ten-seater motor boat made its way gently through the silent River Das. The river was flowing eastward. So was Bhagath Lavanya Shekhar and the other nine passengers. Bhagath was out and alive, after a gruelling war of acting in the dust and heat with as many as 200 people, on and off screen. He had a month's off from the hectic schedule. The second season shoot preps would begin next month. So, he had to ready himself. And even though his home was only a three-hour journey away from the shooting location in the Little Film Studio within Kolaazham Film Development Corporation's 2000-acre property, the agreement stipulated that Bhagath be present for the whole 165 days of the second season's planned shooting days. There were breaks allowed in between, but for the most part Bhagath was living in that hell called The Rhino Emperor. Jaseela, his long-time friend Akbar's daughter had given Bhagath a revival, a forgotten star of Kollywood, akin to the phoenix bird's rise from the ashes. But Bhagath was a changed man now. During his heyday, yes, he was much interested in fame, money, women and liquor. He bothered about the screenplays less as long as he got his fat paycheque and beautiful women to romance. But all those interests lead to his downfall and eventual ousting from the film field. Nowadays he just wanted to live quietly with his wife and daughters and make amends with his sister who was still not sure about him. He hated the fact about being born to his parents in private but had to boast about how lucky he was to have such parents, in all the interviews. The public knew nothing about his dire predicament.

But, Jaseela knew the calibre of this fifty nine year old man. And Bhagath knew from the start, how legendary Akbar's daughter would become one day. And that one day had arrived around two years back when for apparently no reason Bhagath applied for a screen test for The Rhino Emperor's titular character, upon the advice of Jaseela. These Europeans. They wanted a screen test for anyone willing to act in the big budget series. Screen test?? Bhagath scoffed at the idea. The two-time National Award winner knew in his heart, he could pull off the best performance if he was given a decent screenplay to work with. The Rhino Emperor was exactly that. A performance of a lifetime. This time, it was not the paycheque, but the power and the scale of the character Jeyopola that drew Bhagath to Jaseela's dream project.

Another thing was the Sony handycam Bhagath had given to Jaseela back in 2008 when she was loitering near his caravan. Back then, the hot-tempered superstar was known to whack the brains out of any fan who would dare to touch even the dust stuck on Bhagath's caravan. But it was the dear Jaseela. Bhagath's manager Shofi brought the teenage girl inside the caravan. Jaseela felt scared seeing the superstar, sans his hair wig. Bhagath enquired lovingly, "What is it my dear Jaseela? No school today?" to which came the reply "No uncle Bhagath. I am having stomach pain. So amma brought me to this set." Her eyes automatically trailed off towards a camera being placed on charge. There was a glittering shine in her eyes. Bhagath saw that. "Akbar tells me you like films. What do you like my dear? To act?". Jaseela responded enthusiastically saying, "No uncle, I wish to become a writer and director. And maybe make you my lead in a film one day." That was sixteen years ago.

When Jaseela's call came, and when Bhagath reached her office to meet with her two years ago, on her office shelf was that very Sony handycam he had gifted her sixteen years back. Bhagath had purchased it from Japan. He remembered that trip. His wife was with him. She was carrying at that time. On their return flight, the airplane had to pass through an air pocket which shook the airplane violently. And as a consequence, Soumya and her superstar husband lost their unborn, unseen child, their first if that child was born. Soumya had conceived after almost eleven years of treatment. And it was Bhagath's insistence that she travel with him to Japan. It was six months into the pregnancy. But the gods had other plans. Now, they had two daughters, Srividya and Sridhanya, both studying in the UK. What memories simply rush into one's mind upon glancing at an object. That handycam brought happiness and sadness to Bhagath as he sat there, in Jaseela's office listening to the exploits of the power-hungry king, the old Jeyopola.

And, the screen test was a success. Jonathan loved Bhagath in Jeyopola's role. Bhagath came in wearing the prosthetic of a wobbly stomach. Jeyopola's fat bulging stomach was the symbol of his greed for power. This tyrant's role was Jaseela's guru dakshina, as she is quoted to have said, to her mentor Bhagath garu. But the bulging stomach was a problem when it came to enacting the love making scenes of which there were many, written in the screenplay. Bhagath felt ashamed of stripping his clothes in front of young women and 'performing' the making out scenes. The junior artists, many of whom were college students and in for quick money and possible fame, had no qualms in stripping their dresses in front of a crew. After all, the series was helmed by a woman. So, there would be safety. Jaseela was completely satisfied with the way the college girls acted their parts, that of the mistresses of king Jeyopola.

But, for Bhagath, it was indeed a very tough time. He liked the character a lot. In fact, his former days as a flamboyant and arrogant actor was this character who happened to be older, that's all. It would be like a cake walk to act out the cruelties of this tyrant on screen. And boy was it a delight during the screen test to see Bhagath unleash Jeyopola onto the onlookers. Even Jaseela, the creator, felt a fear run down her spine during a particular scene's screen test in which Jeyopola cut off a spy's scrotum. Or even if it was the sword bearing scenes done for the screen test, the tyrant king was ever present. All that raw power was visible. But it would take a lot of coercing and clever words to make Bhagath agree to do the love scenes, or even the lip locks with the young women doing the mistress roles. Distress was running high. Jaseela had to do something to make Bhagath work in the bed scenes. Either she had to cut off those scenes, which would then receive huge backlash from the younger section of the audiences, or she would have to devise a strategy to make Bhagath do the job.

A visibly tired Bhagath hopped off the boat and started walking onto the top of the walkway atop River Das. A kilometre away was the iconic Nothing Park. There, he would have some relief from the frantic fans who were beginning to recognise Jeyopola's breather of life. And surprisingly it was the womenfolk who actually accosted Bhagath for selfies or autographs. The menfolk were either jealous or logical. God knows what. Bhagath entertained none of the fans. But he was polite as could be, as that too was stipulated in the agreement: Not to be arrogant with the fans, but be polite. And Bhagath simply became the beacon of politeness. The Rhino Emperor's first season's massive success propelled Bhagath into superstardom, which he abhorred personally.

Nothing Park. Bhagath took in a load of fresh air. He circulated his being with that load of fresh air and let it out for the trees to suck the expelled air in. This barter system, exchanging airs, continued for almost three hours. Bhagath forgot that time was ticking away. He sat somewhere, where there was the head of a Buddha statue. The rest of the statue might be in Angkor Wat, thought Bhagath. Now, at this part of the silent Nothing Park, there was the Buddha's head, Bhagath, an old woman reading the Bhagavad Gita, an energetic squirrel running around and some pigeons. Lucky fellow thought Bhagath, as no one at this spot recognised him. But that old lady reminded him of his own mother, Lavanya Shekhar. Oh, how he despised his mother. She was alive and well. That was not the matter. Each time he appeared on some mediocre interview program, he had to dole out words matching with the thoughts of the audience. He had to sing praises of how lucky it was for him to be born the son of the late industrialist Shekhar Hembore and the yesteryear film star

Lavanya Shekhar.

Even coming into acting was never in Bhagath's mind. It was his mother who wanted her legacy, which was self-made mind you, be furthered by Bhagath and his children. When Soumya lost their first child, the continental rift between the celebrity mother and celebrity son escalated sky high. Lavanya wanted her son to divorce his wife. He wouldn't. That was the precise moment when he realised how deeply he loved his wife. At that moment, he decided to step down from films and go away. Bhagath and Soumya went to Tamil Nadu and settled there. But none of this rift was known to the public. There, he was the lucky son of two greats. He was a role model for the children to take care of their parents. Bhagath was even the brand ambassador of the central government's initiative to safe keep the interests of the old generation of the nation.

Bhagath scoffed. He felt disgusted when during a film shooting in his early days, a young actress was asked to go into Bhagath's room to entertain him. He was the kind who never feared from asking women directly if they would sleep with him. He didn't require a middle man. But here the middle man, rather middle woman, was keen on cementing her son's reputation as the next star. And that film required this young actress. But the cunning mother twisted it so hard, the young woman had no choice but to be a toy in Bhagath's hands. But instead, Bhagath asked her hand in marriage. At that very instant. It was not any love for the poor woman, but an angry retaliation against his 'loving' mother. That retaliation stood the test of time; Soumya had been with him ever since. Through every possible flaming arrow of hurt thrown by fate.

Even now, upon exiting the film set, Bhagath made his first call to his wife. He was so excited to hear her voice.

She was equally excited to hear her husband's voice. The excitement now tripled when Bhagath heard his sweety pie, Srividya's voice, over the phone. She had arrived last night. Soumya, Srividya and Sridhanya were flying in, the next morning.

CHAPTER V

Srividya

Srividya Amol was the second of three children born to the Amol Christeena couple. They, her parents and siblings, died when she was four years old. Srividya had both Christ and Krishna as her great friends from her childhood. Not that she was a devout religious person, yet she felt that she had the advantage of seeking answers to queries from two forces rather than one. In that way she was clear cut in her vision for all the days ahead. Srividya was an engineering student, a Kuchipudi dancer and a part time car washer at a nearby car wash operated by her boyfriend, the rapper Y'allmond. His real name was Nithish, from Kerala.

Srividya loved the idea of hard work and sweat. She was in awe with her own mentality regarding work. Yes, money was a factor. But Srividya wanted to keep on remaining active. She cared almost to nil about her physical self. She would clean her body daily. She kept her long hair tidy. But, no nail polish, no threading the eyebrows, and there wasn't much to shave off from her hands and legs. And Y'allmond loved her for that. Nithish was a self-proclaimed hippie rapper kind of dude. He would always be on the go. The couple met only a few times in a month. Yet, the relationship was strong.

One day, while cleaning a car, Srividya felt an uneasy sensation, as though a male's gaze was x-raying through her dress. A few minutes went by. And then, Srividya turned to the male. To her surprise it was a female. There was a male close to the female, but he was reading a book, now that Srividya noticed. The startled female pitched in, "Hi

Srividya. Did I offend you in some manner?". "Yes, very much ma'am. There is already much irritable gaze coming from men. And now from women too?? Don't you have a life!!". Srividya didn't notice her voice rising high. The reader of the book told the female to better explain the situation. The situation was, Srividya was offered a role in a television series' second season which would soon be purchased by an international ott platform. Would she be interested in taking the part?

"But what is the part?", enquired the confused Srividya. "Here is my card. My name is Wendy. I am a casting director. I had seen your dance performance in Thevangal High School where my son is studying. I was quite surprised to see that graceful dancer clean my car right now. I am sorry if my looking at you, my gaze, offended you", said Wendy in a tone of excuse. "Oh, you did offend me madam... But, why me for this role?".

Wendy and the reader male rode off in Wendy's car. Srividya tapped the visiting card given to her. She read through the words in the card. 'Wendy Micheal, Casting Director, Jaseela Productions, Tramway Avenue, Kolaazham West' read the card. Was this some sort of scam? Each time Srividya looked at the designation, the term casting couch sprang up. That frightened her. Was this Wendy some member of a human trafficking group or something? Would that lady sell her to some rich Asian or American drug lord? Nonsense. Said the search engine into which Srividya fed the name Wendy Micheal. The details were there. A genius in finding talent, in short, was this lady Wendy. And so narrowed down was Srividya's thoughts on casting and such, that she forgot Jaseela Productions. Shit!! Now that was real shit. Srividya had always wanted to meet Jaseela, the brain behind a string of women centric hit films. And here, Srividya may have got a chance to work in... wait a minute... The Rhino Emperor!! That huge, sexy saga about humans, love and deceit. Will she get to play a femme fatale? Will she get to smooch someone on screen? How'bout steamy scenes? Will she have to do some sort of belly dance?

Only the first query posed an excitement in Srividya. The rest were pure horrible thoughts. Srividya had never wanted to be in films or the entertainment industry. The only time she came in front of the camera was when Y'allmond made his debut rap song video. He wanted a mingling of the west and the east. So, Srividya donned her Kuchipudi get up and make-up and danced for that video. Other than that, she wasn't inclined on anything related to entertainment. With no parents or relations to ask for guidance, Srividya turned to her mobile phone. She dialled her Nithish. A woman picked the call. "Hello Srividya?", said the woman. Taken a bit aback recognising the voice, Srividya asked if Nithish was there. The reply came that he had run out to buy a pack of condoms. An erotic giggle ensued.

Srividya left the car wash building with her backpack. Srividya felt deeply disturbed. That building was her haven, her resort after college, the practice kendra for her Kuchipudi sessions, the only place where she felt any form of ownership. Srividya met and fell in love with Nithish while staying in an orphanage in Kerala. The church management had organised arts and culture classes in which Srividya decided to learn Kuchipudi for some unknown reason. Nithish had learnt Bharatanatyam. He didn't take his practices further with that. But, Srividya still learned and performed her favourite dance form. By her own definition, Srividya loved to be a woman. She liked her periods, though painful. She liked to be timid, but if someone did impose upon her, they were up for sale in the next meat market. She liked to cry; it was a soothing meditation for her. But she hadn't allowed the gods or fate to dictate her life.

An orphan she was but that wasn't to stop her from being anything. Marriage or kids was not there yet in the cards. After all, Srividya was only 21. She had more to do in Kuchipudi. She wanted a doctorate in Kuchipudi. She wanted to start her own dance school. She loved children. She loved Nithish. Even after that call, Srividya was not willing to blame Nithish for the cheating. They didn't have sex for about four months because Srividya had been practising a hell lot for that performance in Thevangal High School where many stalwarts from the dance field would take part. What if any one of them took notice of this woman? What if any one of them took this woman under their wings? These thoughts made Srividya push her limits. She inadvertently pushed Nithish's limits as well. After all he was a human being. Like any emotion, he would like his sexual thirst to be filled. He found his fill with that woman whose voice was familiar. Srividya didn't blame him. Nor could she blame herself. Kuchipudi for her was everything.

Sitting at the bus stop in the middle of the night, Srividya didn't know what to do. A bus was coming. It was going to Kolaazham West. The bus would be passing Tramway Avenue. Srividya signalled for the bus to stop.

CHAPTER VI

Udit

It was Udit who had dropped Jaseela twice at the airport, for her travels to Dubai and the UK for her meetings with Jonathan. In many ways Udit was Jaseela's confidante. He knew her in and out. She let him know her in and out. After, no, even before her marriage and through the failing marriage and post the divorce, Udit was there like a strong pillar for Jaseela to cling to. Was there some sort of love between the two? No one could say. They never felt any romance for each other. Maybe they were antidotes for each other, a kind even the doctors couldn't prescribe. Now he was waiting at the Shri Raja Raja Khollaram International Airport, waiting for Jaseela who had arrived from her narration of The Rhino Emperor's second season's first episode. Udit was so eager to see Jaseela and feel her warmth.

When Udit explained with a lump in his throat about the harrowing experience he had at the Kolaazham Equator Hotel some weeks back, in that room with Sanu Kumar and Sheikh Ali where they mocked his home which was Asha Ghat and his mother for having danced amongst a hundred junior artists for a livelihood, Jaseela was in Dubai. Sheikh Ali was her cousin from some distant relation. She called up that heartless asshole, added Sanu making it a conference call and she barraged them with insane dialogues that they both didn't show their faces to Udit for another year straight. No one dared to mess with Jaseela. She knew how to deal with people from tinsel town.

Jaseela was among the few film personalities who never sold her heart and soul upon entering that glitz and glam field. Udit respected that trait in her. Jaseela was Udit's one year senior at Pune Film Institute. They had made student films together, ate noodles from the same plate while stranded in a heavy downpour, in a leaking old tea shop somewhere in Assam during one of their trips to scout locations for Jaseela's short film's exterior shots. They even slept on the same bed, but never coinciding their bodies. Udit liked it when Jaseela passed wind. Sometimes the ripping would last at least 8 seconds. And then they both would laugh till their stomachs pained. Udit's bottom would suddenly pitch in. And then the laughter would simply escalate. He could only muster 5 seconds.

Once, Jaseela saw Udit emerge from the bathroom naked. It was so natural that she never saw anything awkward in that. Neither did he. "I think I'll marry you someday Jaseela", said Udit one day. He continued, "You are the kind of person to grow old with." Jaseela felt amused. A mischievous look figured in her eyes. She said, "Yes, someone to grow old and fart loudly with." And the duo just laughed hard. Then Jaseela said, "Look Udit, I love sex. And I haven't stopped having it. Just waiting for the right men. Surely a guy like you shouldn't get locked for life with a woman like me." To which Udit replied, "Have sex with all the right men you want, Jaseela. Just don't give your heart to them. Keep that for me. I love you no matter what."

The gutsy Jaseela felt defeated. She had fallen in love with Udit since their days in the institute, all those years back. But Udit was always different. He never talked about women in a demeaning manner. He had the utmost respect for even the seniors who ragged him, resulting in a broken nose. Jaseela punched one of her classmates who had ragged him. She was in love with Udit, that *incorruptible* being. Udit was the only male in front of whom Jaseela would often feel fear. She was always looking for Udit's approval. She wanted Udit so badly. He was the kind of guy to be married to. And Udit had defeated her here. He proposed first. He had even told her to go her ways but to return to him. Whenever possible. All this happened during the initial location scouting of The Rhino Emperor's first season.

"Maybe you should ask her rather than pester me with your doubts, Wendy", said Udit who just glanced at the young woman cleaning Wendy's car. That one look was enough for him to realise Wendy's uncanny ability to spot a talent. Here was Himsha the seductive dark-skinned mistress of Jeyopola cleaning Wendy's car. It all took maybe two seconds. And Udit was back gorging the new book he got from the series' main D.O.P Heyson Prasanna. It was Sidney Lumet's book on his experiences in film making. Udit was awestruck the first time he saw Twelve Angry Men. Twelve men just talking, inside a room. That was more ambitious than any massive budgeted film from any language he had seen till date. One day Udit too would make a film, maybe about lovers... na... some other topic. But that film would be about people in a single location.

"I think I love Jonathan, Udit. I think I want to have kids with him. What do you think?", tested Jaseela looking keenly at her man.

"Do as you please darling Jaseela. In the end though, come back to me."

"You would be an idiot to wait for me. There are several women out there! Try to find love my dear. I can't lose you to some bullshit intoxication. You know that."

"I have been thinking about that, you know, about other women. I might give it a try. But my heart is where it ought to be."

"How cliched is romance Udit."

"Not at all. Do you see me weeping, or getting drunk when you talked about your feelings to Jonathan? Please don't lower my love's quality Jaseela."

"Ha ha ha... I wonder how the audience will view a love relation like this on screen. I mean there is nothing to lose. Nothing at stake. There is prior agreement between the two people. They can go their separate ways but must return when the impulse has reached its peak."

"Maybe you should include our love story, this monotonous love story, in the second season."

"Yes... Yes, Udit. Jeyopola's estranged daughter Shemer. She can have an affair. It needn't be tumultuous. It can be serene. Like ours."

"Ours is not serene Jaseela. Ours is non-toxic... I don't know how this can be translated onto screen but it's worth a try. One draft can be attempted. I can help you."

"Is that even needed to be said, Udit? I need you in this."

The conversation stopped. The load shedding in that area had just started. Under the bright moonlight, the duo just kept staring at each other. Now, their faces started to come closer and closer. As their lips were about to lock, Udit said, "Kiss my cheeks. Lips later." He immediately turned his face. And Jaseela, in that same momentum pressed her lips onto his cheeks. Annoyed, Jaseela slapped Udit's shoulder. Udit laughed. Seeing Udit laugh, Jaseela followed suit. A few seconds later a voice from below yelled out "Come down Jaseela and Udit. Dinner is ready." "That is mother. Come", said Udit. The duo got up, brushed off the dust from their dresses and walked towards the terrace door. Just then, out of the blue, at the terrace door Jaseela pulled an unsuspecting Udit towards her. She started kissing him passionately. Finally, Udit gave in. He then tied his hands around her waist and professed his gargantuan love for Jaseela collected in his heart over all those long years, and returned the kiss with double the romance and energy that she put in.

Once their wet lips parted ways, their torsos remained together. Jaseela was panting. Udit was excited. At that moment, with a brimming smile on her face, Jaseela said, "I love you Udit. Not Jonathan. I love you…"

CHAPTER VII

Jonathan

Jonathan Meg was a theatre person. He was a professional, a *no surprises* guy, the person who had it all planned. He wanted to be on stage. He wanted to perform, to act. His portrayal of King Lear was the talk of the town back in 1998 when he was just 24 years old. He still had the photo of that night, of his portrayal, in his study at home. It was during the party following the drama that he had met his future wife, Elsa Wittern. Elsa was the third daughter of Sir Ernest Elfway Wittern and Mrs Judith Ernest Wittern. Ernest was among the stalwarts of British cinema. And apparently, he was quite impressed with the young man's take on King Lear. Being a parent of three daughters, perhaps Ernest saw much similarity with Lear. He loved the young lad instantly. Jonathan was a professional. Always planned in advance. He hated surprises.

Over the next few months, as planned by Jonathan, the old man and the young man got to know each other. Jonathan would often visit Ernest's home. He would stay several nights in Ernest's home. On one such night, Ernest even saw in the darkest of the midnight hours, his young child Elsa steal into Jonathan's room. Ernest felt ashamed to have placed his ears on the door, only to hear his daughter and Jonathan moan from deep physical pleasure. Ernest heard Elsa whisper 'a little further up my darling'... Ernest did not know his youngest child had grown old enough. That sudden realisation and the shame of having eavesdropped, led to Jonathan and Elsa joining their hands in holy marriage. Jonathan hated surprises.

The Oscar and Bafta winning actor Sir Ernest probably saw his younger self in the professional Jonathan, that he would take his son-in-law to the major film studios of the time. Jonathan, the fast learner that he was, quickly got to understand the tricks of the film industry. And one day, during breakfast Jonathan announced to his parents-in-law thus, "I am going to start a new production company father and mother. It will be named Little Further Up."

The piece of meat that Ernest had placed in his mouth slipped to his throat and he choked. That shame returned. But Ernest never said anything about *that* night or that shame to his wife. And while he lay to rest forever in the family church graveyard, Little Further Up was gearing up for its first English television series. The theatre prodigy son-in-law took over the estates and assets of his parents-in-law and became a millionaire overnight. Jonathan never forgot his wife's family though. He gave everyone their needed share, put his mother-in-law in a luxurious old age care centre and helped Elsa in producing three beautiful children.

Jonathan loved his children. The eldest was Lisa, now 18 years old. She had a boyfriend. The celebrity that Jonathan was, he was always worried about his daughter. He felt the pain that Ernest must have felt when he flirted around with Elsa. He cared for his children but the twenty six year old marriage of him to Elsa was failing. It was not a surprise to Jonathan. Elsa was someplace else with someone else. And Jonathan was in one of the luxury suites of the Mumbai Equator Hotel, looking at the naked Jaseela who was now getting up from her chair. As she moved past the bed, Jonathan sprang from the bed onto Jaseela. Jaseela shrieked. Soon her lips were covered by Jonathan's. They kissed. But now, only Udit was in Jaseela's mind. She gently pushed Jonathan aside and walked to the shower. Jonathan followed suit. Jonathan greedily forced Jaseela into making love in the steaming shower. Jonathan remarked, "I could make love to you for a whole day Jaseela, like a single shot". Jaseela who now knew it was time for her to completely stop her sexual encounters with Jonathan and other men, stood still suddenly. Her eyes bulged in a eureka moment. Jonathan stood confused. He asked, "Have you grown tired of me?"

"Jonathan... You just gave me the idea of a lifetime", snapped a jubilant Jaseela.

"... Which is?"

Not waiting to respond to Jonathan, Jaseela ran out from the shower, water dripping onto the marble floor. She dashed towards her mobile phone that was lying on the bed. Not caring about the wetness on her body, she jumped onto the springy bed, grabbed the phone and dialled a number. Just as the call got picked on the other side, Jaseela screamed in excitement, "The opening shot of Jeyopola entering the defeated kingdom of Chaapikia will be filmed in a single long duration shot. One long, long duration single shot!! Yes, I'll be coming in two days' time. You must come to pick me. Ok bye."

Closing the shower, with a disgraced face, Jonathan too came out from the shower. Water was dripping from his body. Jonathan was angry, he felt really insulted. He said, "Let me get this straight. You want hundreds of extras, some twenty odd elephants, several horses and all the emotions of the actors and their various movements to various spots in the set to be done in a single shot?? Why didn't you let *me* know about your sudden spark first Jaseela?"

"I have absolutely no idea Jonathan", came the answer, very excited and confident. There was only cinema in Jaseela's eyes now. At that moment Jonathan knew his thing for Jaseela had ended. He was not a tyrant producer. But he needed to be in the game. No prior decision was to be made without his consideration. He wouldn't impede the creative process. But, Jaseela's epiphany, in the middle of their shower sex, was totally unprofessional. For her to simply brush him off and blurt her spark to someone else before letting him know, the fund provider, was more than Jonathan could take. Jaseela could have suggested the idea to the whole team while they were having their team dinner or during the screenplay discussion with the execs the next day. The bed was not the right spot. But how could he voice his concern right now? Here was this sumptuous woman just fallen off his hands, he had barely begun to enjoy. And by all chances, she was in an affair with someone else. Jonathan hated that surprise twist. He hated that 'single shot' idea more. That had to be nipped, and fast... The destructive ending had just begun.

Jaseela left the suite that evening happy with the epiphany. Jonathan made a video call to his operations manager Tim.

"Morning from London Jon. You look spent. Well spent."

The men laughed. Then,

"Yeah... The writer/director is a real game I tell you my friend. Oh that curvy body."

"God you are one lucky swine you bastard... Hey, is this some kind of ritual or something?"

"I guess so... Seems she gets good or great ideas after we make love. But that's going to stop soon."

"Hey there seems to be an undercurrent of some sort of drama that happened. Wanna talk Jon?"

"She wants a single shot", said Jonathan wiping his face with his palms and heaving a sigh.

"You mean for the ending scene?"

"Exactly."

"Oh my... That is... That is a massively bold move man. Too expensive as well."

"And that's why we won't proceed with that idea of Jaseela's. I want you and our team to fly down to Kolaazham next week. You need to be present for the screenplay discussion scheduled with the crew, next week. The scene can stay. It is raw. But, not the single shot."

"Well from what I gather from the bits and pieces you have spoken about that scene; it can create cinematic history Jon."

"Don't bother about histories and legacies. My money must be spent the way I want it to be spent."

Tim nodded in agreement. For almost a whole week, the overthinking Jonathan invested in Jaseela, into her sudden obsession for the single shot, their flopped shower sex, and Jaseela's possible affair with someone all made Jonathan so frustrated and angry. He gave excuses to stay away from the team meetings. He didn't want to see Jaseela anymore. He was sure Jaseela knew Jonathan didn't like surprises at the professional level. And she did just that. One Sunday afternoon, in a resort in Ooty, Wendy came into the bed from the washroom. Glancing at the moody Jonathan she said, "She is in love with Udit. She'll stop giving you her body during the upcoming episode writing sessions. Am I not better than her?"

"If she is a whirlpool Wendy, you are a tsunami", remarked Jonathan as he immersed himself into her.

CHAPTER VIII

Crew

With less than a year before the shooting was set to commence, Jaseela called in her crew first, for the initial screenplay discussion. Inputs from the technicians were of supreme significance to these period sagas.

Roopa Dutt was the first person Jaseela pulled into the crew. Being a busy intimacy coordinator, Jaseela had to make sure Roopa was signed as quickly as possible. And with the second season having more sex and physical violence, Roopa's presence was of paramount importance. The last season had Ashna Swamy. She parted due to pregnancy complications. Roopa was given a detailed idea of the script and the critical ending scene of the second season's first episode which would be a single shot. That one scene was going to break everyone, especially Roopa who had to make sure that her actors were really comfortable in performing their assigned tasks. Roopa needed a session with the actors, which was readily granted by Jaseela. Roopa went off to meet her actors and work with them, one to gain their trust in her work and two to build a trust among themselves.

Kumar S Pillai, Jaseela's close friend of twenty years, had been entrusted to continue his job with the set design. He was the Production Designer. His was a team of 70 artists and construction workers. Kumar had a major role to do. He had to do major revamps to the already massive set constructed on the Little Pictures compound. One of the toilets, cleverly placed behind a market piece, had plumbing problems. With at least 500 hundred people on set during shooting days, it would definitely be Kumar's and team's duty to make sure everyone went to attend nature's call safely, especially the womenfolk.

He showed a 3D design of the improved set that would sit on 260 acres. The set had a lavish palace, a lake made to look like a sea, a beach, a battle ground, a courtroom, a harem, a large swimming pool that heated the water, a river, a forest, a village, an arena near the beach, huts for the actors and the in-house doctor etc. The highlight was any of these could be disassembled and reassembled to suit any improvisation that was needed on the spot, in less than two hours. The toilets were improved, a huge dining area was seamlessly designed into the set, recreational and resting spots were arranged in select areas of the set. The only condition for the set was that it had to feel fictional. There shouldn't be any reference to say the Viking era or any of the European types. Jaseela wanted something on the lines of a Mughal period town. Kumar's set design needed some tweaking on that part. Jaseela gave the approval for the construction to begin.

Heyson Prasanna was the new recruit into the team. In the first season Jaseela herself handled the camera. But that was a less daunting task as compared to the second season which would be more ambitious in scale and emotions. Heyson went through the entire first season and jotted down his findings. Jaseela had overused the Dutch shot. Even for a few romantic scenes! Pff!! The first thing Heyson said when he joined as Director of Photography was to avoid that tilted shot as far as possible. He wanted the audience to experience the scenes in their eye level itself. While usually everyone gave Jaseela comments wrapped in colourful words, Heyson gave no shit. He said what he felt. Jaseela liked the young man's commanding voice. Having the task of, a huge burden, of pulling off a single shot that included the camera to dangle at least 150ft above ground then to shoulder level then to floor level, all while moving between several animals and men and locations was beginning to haunt Heyson within, though he sought not to show it outside. What was haunting him more was the money he was offered by Tim to back out from this series. He so badly wanted to be part of The Rhino Emperor. He wanted to pull off the gargantuan single shot. But he was to be paid only Rs 15 Lakhs per episode for the second season's six episodes. Tim had offered Rs 1.5 Cr to back out. Heyson agreed to leave right before the principal photography was to begin.

Wendy and Jaseela were room-mates back in the institute. Wendy wanted to be a scenarist. But then love struck her. And she relegated herself to becoming a loving home-maker. But, when the sudden death of her husband occurred, Wendy had no means of survival in front of her. Jaseela took her and the tiny little kids in. She fine-tuned that critical aspect evident in Wendy, spotting talent. Wendy fell in love with her late husband knowing well that he could cook, even when she hadn't tasted a morsel of what he made. She was correct. Wendy also helped with the screenplay writing. Ever since Wendy came into the film business, she found work. But mostly she stuck with Jaseela. Jaseela too wanted Wendy with her. Wendy and Jaseela; the gal pals. It's not that Jaseela didn't notice that same cologne smell coming from Wendy, but she didn't have the time to question her on that. Maybe Wendy had the same cologne. Actually, she didn't. She was sleeping with Jonathan. That fellow made sure she felt heaven. Wendy craved a man's physical presence. Jonathan gave that. He was also tuning her into becoming the writer/

director of the second and possibly the third and final season. Why not? Several scenes in the first season had Wendy's creative touch in them. She could write and direct. Direction was always there in her mind. During their sex, Jonathan pounded Wendy like a hammer hitting on a nail. And Wendy soon forgot about Jaseela's kind heart. She embraced Jonathan and his vicious idea of her taking the hit television series forward.

Fathima Maqbool was Shaikh Ali's wife. And even though Jaseela fired at Ali and made him promise to never appear in front of her ever again, she had a huge love for this woman. Being a cancer survivor, having removed both her breasts, Fathima still found solace in her modest stitching venture. What Jaseela loved most was Fathima's interest in researching attires from various times and incorporating them into the dresses of today. The other day, Fathima had made a saree that was modelled on a female Viking. That was a marvellous piece. Jaseela decided to wear that saree for The Rhino Emperor's Season 2 launch ceremony. But right now, Fathima and her team of thirty members needed to design and stitch almost a thousand dresses of various types, for the saga. And Fathima with her assistant Joby, showed Jaseela an album full of drawings of the attires of the characters of the saga's season two. Only three designs needed a slight tweaking. The rest were approved instantly.

Padmashri Devaprasad Rai was Jaseela's go-to regarding the music, for the songs, the bgm and the sound design. All sorts of music for every possible human emotion had to be created from scratch. And every music had to feel ancient yet contemporary. The theme music of The Rhino Emperor was a smash hit among the burgeoning fans of the television show that even the grand old musician of Indian cinema felt quite intimidated at the prospect of composing music for Jaseela's mammoth. But in the months to follow, Devaprasad did compose at least 70 music tracks according to Jaseela's vision. Jaseela liked the seductive music associated with Himsha the best. Somehow Udit's face and body filled her mind whenever she heard that music. It was not an erotic sensation. Rather, that music rightfully evoked Himsha's state of mind. One of the most sensitive characters in the show, Himsha was in the villainous grasp of Jeyopola. She longed to go home. She was tired of having to sleep with several men when Jeyopola ordered. Himsha was in fact the representative of every common person watching that show. Devaprasad Rai, a man who in his younger days had deep love for a prostitute but couldn't bring it to fruition due to societal pressures, had that long-lost love in mind while composing Himsha's tune. He later opened up about that to Jaseela. He deliberately avoided talking about Tim's offer though. He had shown Tim the middle finger. He loved Jaseela like a daughter. But she needn't know about that offer now.

The prosthetics department was being handled well by Smitha Preetham. Smitha had been a cake maker. It was Udit who brought her in to meet Jaseela once. Smitha had brought Udit's head, an exact replica, in cake form to Jaseela. This was five years ago. The trio still remembered the violent shriek Jaseela let out when she saw Udit's head on a platter. So heavily impressed by Smitha's craftsmanship, Jaseela sent Smitha to Hollywood to learn more about prosthetics. And boy, the number of perfect severed heads, legs and hands she made for season one. Smitha simply had to repeat that for the coming season as well. She and her team of twelve people.

Stunt co-ordinator Lucky Singh Rajput and his team had just a year to come up with a way to make the old wobbly Jeyopola fight. It shouldn't be a mockery or mimicry. Genuine fight. After all, Jeyopola was a king. He ought to know how to wield the sword. Luckily for Lucky, Bhagath was all game about learning to wield the sword once again. But with the wobbly stomach, that was an uphill task. A back injury was probable. They had to devise new methods and contraptions to not burden Bhagath. Lucky also had to recruit nearly 300 junior artists exclusively as the soldiers. He had to train them, get almost a thousand armours, shields, swords and all the whatnots ready in less than a year. For now, wooden swords would do. But metallic swords and other stuff needed to be produced faster than planned. Neither Tim nor Jonathan went to that department.

The series film editor Mitra Saha didn't make much of an appearance. She was literally sunk in the almost 2500 rushes of the war shots between Jeyopola and Walika, from which she had to stitch and sew a war sequence that lasted around 25-30 minutes. She was sitting in her studio in Chennai and toiling every day for the past three weeks to cut and place the war sequence. Only ten minutes of the war had been successfully placed. Either Jaseela or Mitra would find some shortcoming in the editing, some emotion missing there, some comment or verbal fight over the selection of a shot when the previous one was better etc. Mitra had won the Indian Television Academy Award last year for Best Editor. Her cuts were precise. She hated the non-linear style of storytelling. So did Jaseela. Now, as the second season's first episode's second major part was gearing up for shoot, Mitra had to speed up the mega war scene's edits. Jaseela kept Mitra on her toes.

Operations Manager of Little Further Up, Tim Cacy, the confidante of Jonathan, was making a note of all the possible setbacks that could occur during the production of this mammoth television series. Tim single-handedly made the entire accounts in a week's time. He knew the exact budget required for the second season. He still had to figure in the catering service. No one had taken interest this time to cook for Jaseela's series as during the shoot of the first season, some ugly fights broke out between her crew and the then catering team which then led to all the catering services registered with the union boycotting the shoot of The Rhino Emperor. Jaseela now knew that getting someone to cook for her huge team was a bigger task than doing that colossal single shot. Smitha had offered a suggestion. It was kept a secret for now.

"So, guys, we have just four months in front of us. And there will be many days wherein you'll need to go home to your family. I won't stop that. But I want the jobs assigned to be done on a war footing. You all know that with this season we are stepping up the ante. The stakes, as in the story, are also high for us in reality as well. We need to keep working with our brains and bodies to keep this juggernaut rolling. So... as you all are aware the last season ended with king Jeyopola winning against his enemy Walika. We had stopped the season with Jeyopola inviting his new mistress Himsha into his chamber. That time, only the back was shown. Now, we have selected a young lady and luckily, she fits the bill and luckily, she has agreed to play the part of the emotionally subdued yet immensely sexy Himsha. You know, thinking about the sex in the series, the other day a group of school going teens spotted me at a mall in Delhi. They were ecstatic about the series. One girl among them asked if there would be nude scenes in the new season.

For a second, I felt shocked, I must confess. You know school kids asking such a question. But then, the other attitude would be like what the hell, this can be a kind of understanding of the physical realm for the young genders. So, coming back to the series, the first episode that will be running to around 50 minutes will show a new Jeyopola. New in the sense, he has now become emperor of about 38 provinces including the new addition Chaapikia. So, there is a marked change in his body language. That change needs to reflect in his attire, on the palanquin fitted on the elephant on which he arrives etc... Jeyopola has found the time to change to new clothes and have a quick wash before entering his new win. Here, understand that, our actor Mr Bhagath will act out the changed Jeyopola quite well, but the attire he wears and the way he walks, the angles chosen to capture those changes, changes in the power dynamics, his omnipotent feel, the helplessness of the people around him... all need to be portrayed well. Regarding the hanging of the children, either we can employ three grown-ups who are of the children's height or we can make dummies of the children and hang them. Smitha let me know what you think is better. Heyson seems confused. Don't worry, I'll sit with your department exclusively one day and we will figure it out. And then we will sit with all you guys and discuss the closing or ending shot. It is only after we have an idea can we proceed with the actors. You see now, I want the shot to go like this: we open the scene with a CG shot showing the seaside in Chaapikia. From there the camera flies through the city that Jeyopola will enter soon. The CG stops at the point where our camera begins to shoot; at the feet of several soldiers loitering around for a command. Camera on ground level ok. Their voices can be heard. Be with me here ok. The camera then slowly rises to shoulder level at the same time moving towards a tent. A soldier has to pass by before the camera enters the tent. Within the tent are some women preparing a royal dress. The camera moves to a naked Jeyopola exiting a makeshift shower. We hear two soundings of the horn some minutes apart. Now, his chest and wobbly stomach are bare. We can see his thighs and legs suggesting that he is naked. There is a young woman near him. Jeyopola will be caressing her butt lustfully. At this point, the camera moves out of the tent and into another tent where sits Jeyopola's wife the queen Margafa. She doesn't look happy at all. Her dressing up has finished. Our camera then moves out of the tent to see that the soldiers, horses and the elephants all have been arranged meticulously. Yes, I want it that way. Snap of the finger. Just like that. Come on man imagine it, visualise it baba... Fine... Now comes the tricky part. We need to mount our camera onto a crane or rope and then as the procession begins to march forward the camera must rise above the height of the royal palanquin fitted onto the elephant on which sits Jeyopola and Himsha. And we need to make sure Birbal who plays the defeated king Walika is safely tied to the elephant's hind foot. Yes he is ok with it as long as I buy him two potato oat biriyanis ha ha... Mind you, Birbal has to stay tied till after we have crossed the city wall and till the elephant stops. Now, going back a bit, as the camera exits the queen's tent, by then Bhagath must have hopped into the royal palanquin. No, the stomach stays... Now, using the rope or the crane, the camera must move a bit quickly forward. We can hear the third horn sounding. We can create the dust rising from the massive march using CG. Once the camera enters the city crossing the wall, we lower the camera to shoulder level and move through the dejected faces of the defeated citizens of Chaapikia. We can hear the marching thud in the background..."

A visibly sweating and parched Jaseela ended her speech, the single take speech, and slam dunked onto a seat nearby. Within seconds she dozed off snoring amidst the clapping of the crew.

CHAPTER IX

Attack

Roopa the intimacy coordinator was sitting on the carpeted floor of her studio facing the actors Bhagath, Birbal, Sharmeela, Anju, Mohith, Srividya and several female junior artists who were to play the roles of Jeyopola's mistresses. Dummies of the three children of king Walika's character were decided to be made and placed on the tree branch. So, Roopa didn't call in the child artists. She could see that Bhagath and Sharmeela were really tense. It was they who had the most violent acts to be part of in that crucial ending scene. Roopa started off with a genuine smile and a soothing voice, "Hello all. By now you all will have gone through the ending scene of the new season's episode one. There are more body exposure, sex and violence inflicted on the characters' bodies. We can expect more of these in the coming episodes... I am present here now to discuss with you all those acts. We all will be signing the agreements in a week's time. Is there anyone who feels uncomfortable to be part of this project? You can see that the director and producer are not present here. You can talk to me all you want about your feelings about this project. I can help you get through the acts, or let you and the film makers see common ground and help you, you know, exit the production gracefully. Can we talk?"

Anju raised her hands first. Roopa nodded to proceed. In her mind Anju had wanted to have a mind-blowing sex with Bhagath the moment she knew she was to play his on-screen wife. She liked that guy. She remembered that instant, about a big poster she had of him back in the early

2000s. But he was a family man now. And this was acting. Jaseela had mentioned a sex scene between Jeyopola and Margafa that would be happening in S02E04. Anju said, "I have worked with only a few people. I have very less experience in this industry. But I have been approached in indecent manners by several men. That I do not tolerate. Here anyway, there is an intimate scene between me and Bhagath in the fourth episode. I am not sure if Jaseela has written the complete episode. All I know is it has to be erotic. Margafa is trying to win back her husband. So, I have to take the initiative. I am ok with showing my body till the waist, front and back yes. No, no prosthetics. I want to keep the originality. As regards the body touches, I have a vein problem with my neck. So, touching the neck is a no no. Stomach, upper pelvis, outer thighs and the back, I am comfortable with touches there. Ya I am sure with showing my breasts but no touching. I'm all in regarding liplocks... Ya that's all. I assume you will train us to understand our screen partner better?"

Roopa gave a thumbs up nodding her head in the affirmative. She was truly impressed with Anju's matter of fact talk. Next, Bhagath volunteered.

Bhagath began the talk. He said, "Hello Roopa. I must first of all say that I am really surprised how developed our industry has become. During my heyday there was not the slightest inkling for the need of your post Roopa. Frankly speaking, I even smooched my female lead so hard, on one film set. I got carried away. She cried a lot that day. I told her to get over it. I was a rude brute in the early 2000s. I resent that action now. I kind of hate myself for that. And here, there is the defilement of the defeated queen by my character, and with Srividya, my colleague, a brilliant child and the intimate scene with Anju. Anju, my whole body will be aching with me having to wear an 8 Kg prosthetic stomach all day on set. By the time we shoot episode four, you guys can bury me under the ground hahaha... Is a stand-in possible? I mean I would love to work with Anju for that scene, but I am sceptical about my body. I have even spoken to our stunt master to show me some leniency in the fight scenes. I am 59 years old, you know. And yes, every time I see Srividya I am reminded of my own daughter who bears the same name. I sincerely want to be Jeyopola, and my character can have his mistress. But how can I vision Srividya in that position? Three beautiful women... I need your help, Roopa."

Roopa clapped listening to an award-winning actor open up like that. She felt proud about her job. It was moments like this that gave her an added sense of duty and responsibility, to do her job better. Sharmeela had already felt a sense of protection when she saw Roopa the other day during a ladies only outing of the crew and cast. For the past few years she had taken a break from acting to care for the kids. But, it was Birbal who suggested her name for the queen's character when he was cast as king Walika. There was a sex scene involving the husband and wife in real, as king and queen in reel, just before Walika set out to war against Jeyopola in Season 1. That was a fun scene to do. But here, she was to be dragged, stripped and pounded upon by Bhagath who would be wearing an 8 Kg prosthetic wobbly stomach. She had her apprehensions which she voiced, "What worries me most is the part where my dress will be torn out. Jaseela enquired if I could really show my breasts. That would feel authentic, she says. I don't feel that's right. We can get prosthetic breasts right Roopa?". Roopa nodded in the affirmative. Sharmeela continued, "Bhagath too was asked if he could show his real genitals. Yes, that does add to the horror and disgust to the scene. But, reading Bhagath's face, I know he does not like that either. I think we can tell this to Jaseela. We can create prosthetic or even plastic male genitals right". A visibly surprised Bhagath enquired, "Really? You can do all that now? Hey I feel really old now listening to all this. And thinking that I was away only for around fifteen years." "You see the last season didn't have as much sex or nudity for that matter. And so, Ashna Swamy didn't have the need to use them much. And Sharmeela, tell us, how is your comfort with the characters touching you? It has to feel rough. But we don't want any inadvertent touches", enquired Roopa.

Sharmeela began explaining about which all body parts up to what extent she was ok with the touching. Birbal with his villainous twin character Warika coming in S02E02 and then going full swing throughout the second and third season, was also keen to discuss his doubtful thoughts as Warika was a guy who always enjoyed sitting naked in any company. He was a sex maniac. He was pure disgust. The diametric opposite of Walika. Roopa's expert guidance with Birbal's inputs were a boon to him to mitigate his tensions. A sudden burst of happiness made him kiss his wife who chipped in more than he expected. Everyone clapped watching a real-life romance unfold. Roopa talked with the junior artists set to play the mistresses. Their queries and concerns were duly noted. Without him knowing, Mohith's eyes trailed off to capture a glance of Srividya who was timidly looking at him at that moment. Boy, that was an electrifying second. But, that one second's heavenly feel got disrupted so fast when some masked men suddenly barged into the hall yelling slur words. They slapped Srividya and the other women with her. One of them caught Mohith by the neck and pushed him to the floor. Bhagath got a kick in the stomach. Roopa was beaten badly. Somehow Birbal and Sharmeela were spared. The goons spat the pan they were chewing on to the floor. Their complaint was that a woman was running a sex club in that hall. They broke the windows, the lights, and the available furniture. They ran away.

Jaseela went straight to the police station. She was shocked that an incident like this would happen in Kolaazham, a fairly progressive land. The officer had caught hold of one goon but let him out on bail before Jaseela arrived at the station. She smelled foul play. Udit was in the hospital running around trying to keep the situation calm. Roopa needed to take rest for four weeks. Srividya had a tooth broken. Mohith's throat and neck received severe injuries. One of the junior artists vomited blood. She was kicked in the stomach. Bhagath too vomited blood. The junior artist and Bhagath were kept under supervision for three days.

Jaseela, Udit, Soumya (Bhagath's wife), Srividya (Bhagath's daughter), Heyson, Wendy, Jonathan, Tim, Birbal, Sharmeela, Fathima and Lucky Singh Rajput all assembled at the hospital. The attack was a totally unexpected turn of events. For Jaseela, this shock was too much to bear. She wanted to fly to Canada that very instant. Only Jameela's kids' presence could calm her. But then that would be a selfish escapist thing to do. All the others were here, teary eyed. Jaseela panned her eyes across the dejected faces that stood with her. Jaseela sat on the floor then. She started to cry. A feverish cry. That cry, that tsunami of tears, that overflow of pain and months of nerve wrecking struggle to pull off a creative behemoth had all trickled down into this mindless violence. Udit sat down next to her caressing her hair. None of the really dejected people could notice the slight smirk smeared on the faces of Jonathan and Tim. Wendy cast a glance towards Jonathan. Heyson was caught in the middle. He cared for Jaseela's predicament. But he felt Jonathan's fiery glance burn his shoulder. Heyson stood there, like a statue. Now Jonathan knew who Jaseela's lover was.

Smitha's call came to Udit. She relayed the news that the goons were all missing. They probably escaped soon after the attack. There wasn't much to do. Smitha's voice was shivering. It gave way. She cut the call.

The production stalled for around two whole months. And unknown to none in the crew, Wendy was giving her body to the no-surprises man and pleasing him occasionally. But not known to Jonathan, Wendy began seeing Tim too. With the former, she was waiting to don the director's cap of The Rhino Emperor, as part of the perks. And with the latter, she was in love.

CHAPTER X

Shaping up

The D.O.P Heyson, Casting director Wendy, Jaseela, Production Designer Kumar S Pillai, Udit, Costume Designer Fathima, Intimacy Coordinator Roopa Dutt and several of the crew were present. The still photographer Prasanna Silva, Heyson's father, was clicking the photos of Bhagath in Jeyopola's outfit. Bhagath had to wear an 8 Kg prosthetic stomach fitted with plastic pubic hair, that all wobbled slightly. The stomach was a beautiful creation by the Prosthetics team led by Smitha Preetham. All these people had worked with Jaseela before. And she was comfortable with them. And when The Rhino Emperor's second season began taking its baby steps, Jaseela wanted these talents to continue to grace her project.

That wobbling stomach with the pubic hair was a smash hit. If in the beginning of the first season, king Jeyopola's belly was just beginning to bulge, here in the second season it had bulged completely. That bulge symbolised Jeyopola's greed for power. Thankfully the audience did grasp the symbols Jaseela threw at them. Bhagath was quite excited for the photoshoot as there were no women he needed to embrace. In the photoshoot itself, Bhagath was the ruthless Jeyopola. Next to come was the defeated king Walika played by the eccentric Birbal Shanthan. Birbal had a double role in season two. One, of the king Walika, and the other, his twin brother the cunning Warika. Warika was to make his appearance in the second episode of season two. Jaseela and team were totally taken aback noticing how effortlessly Birbal Shanthan transformed from the defeated man to the cunning man. Bhagath even clapped and hailed Birbal for that transformation. After Birbal came Sharmeela Birbal, who was to play the ill-fated wife of Walika. Sharmeela had to pose in the most dejected manner possible. She just visualised her traumatic childhood when her uncle used to molest her. That was her secret trigger. And her photo session was perfect. She wiped her tears and left the room. Birbal, Udit and Jaseela knew about that trigger.

The semi naked Himsha made everyone roll their eyes. Even the calm and composed Udit couldn't lift his eyes off Srividya. Costume designer Fathima had her team stitch a costume with the same colour as Srividya's semi-dark skin tone. With the bosom, cleavage and even the naval sketched to perfection, Srividya looked very much semi naked in front of the whole crew. Instead of feeling disgust, Srividya felt a form of liberation. She had her reservations when she was told about the character of Himsha. The seductress, the mistress. There would be a lot of lip lock scenes, maybe a few sex scenes. Her pay check would be Rs 65 Lakhs. A wildness in Srividya took hold of her. She agreed to every condition. She wanted to flaunt her body. Srividya wanted to feel free. Anju Leelavathi who played Jeyopola's wife Margafa was next. She took an instant liking to Srividya. And to everyone's surprise, the on-screen rivalry that was set to burn the screens between Margafa and Himsha, would but turn to a close friendship between Anju and Srividya in the later days.

All the major actors came and had their character photo sessions taken. The young heartthrob of the series Mohith Awaan who played Jeyopola's ruthless army general was reprising that role in the second season. Seeing Srividya at the canteen enjoying tea with Anju, he bumped in.

"You are a Kuchipudi dancer right Srividya?". "Yes sir... And you are Mohith Awaan". Srividya felt a slight shock hit her nerves. This man was handsome. His receding hairline only added to his beauty. "Are you done with the flirting Mohith?", enquired Anju laughing. "What... Can't I flirt? She looks beautiful. But awfully talented too. My mom knows Kuchipudi", retorted Mohith who now saw the evening sun caressing the semi dark skin of Srividya. She looked like a goddess now. Srividya could see Mohith's face glow in the evening sun. Anju knew she had better leave the spot for now. She did take out a jibe as she went which was, "Mohith don't take the girl for granted. And Srividya, welcome to tinsel town my dear." Anju left. Some paparazzis barged in somehow and started clicking photos of Srividya. Srividya started to shiver in fright. Noticing that, Mohith suddenly jumped to her side and escorted her into the building. By then the bouncers had pushed the paparazzis out. But they had got what they needed.

Inside, in the conference room, Jaseela was standing near an extreme corner. Udit was close to her. She looked at him. Udit said quietly, "Let it out Jaseela". And with that assurance Jaseela farted gently. That was necessary. She was now going to face the actors and explain her idea about the ending scene of the first episode of the second season of The Rhino Emperor. These guys were sharper than the technicians.

"...Yes, I want the camera to move backwards from the two-shot of Jeyopola and Walika and rise above the ground and keep rising further in parallel with the citizens turning their heads and gasping in unison, some shrieking, as the camera reaches the hanged children. The camera turns almost 180 degrees to capture the lifeless children slowly moving in the breeze. And then the camera drags back to the victorious looking Jeyopola. And all that while we can hear the ecstatic cries of Walika in the background... What was that? See, this is a single long duration shot. And the elephant on which Bhagath is sitting will hopefully bend down for him or his character to get off, at the marked spot. We need to make sure that elephant's mahouts are explained that point properly. Well, if the elephant runs amok, rest assured I'll be the first to escape the film set hahahaha... All right... Now the camera has reached Jeyopola's shoulder level ok. He begins to walk towards the royal hall. I haven't written it, but we need many young women standing on each step and throwing flowers at the king. We will use the good old Steadicam. I love that equipment. Heyson will comply. Now we follow Jeyopola from behind. Jeyopola enters. Now, outside the hall, it is hot. But inside, the hall is designed with a tinge of blue, to indicate the coolness within. Jeyopola feels refreshed instantly, as though he has entered an ac hall. That is evident on his face. A few steps further and he stands like a statue. The focus shifts to the throne bathed in sunlight, some 30 ft away ensconced between two massive pillars. At this point, the camera will rise and take a drone-like shot of the entire massive hall and return to Jeyopola. The massiveness of the hall has to set in... Yes, here Himsha comes and hisses into Jeyopola's ears. As she whispers actually, the camera will zoom in, such that in the frame we see Srividya's lips and Bhagath's ear. Once her whisper is over, immediate zoom out!! And Jeyopola gets angry at Himsha. The camera moves 360 degrees around Jeyopola and Himsha. He pushes her down and then begins the walk towards the throne. We only hear his dress brushing against his body, his shoes sounding on the floor, and the gentle weep of Himsha. The camera follows Jeyopola as he now seats himself on the throne. Here the camera lowers itself and tilts upwards, a worm's eye view, to show an imposing Jeyopola's figure. He has now spread his fatty thighs and slapping one thigh he beckons Himsha. We still stay on Jeyopola and his manic, victorious body language. We can hear Himsha walking now. She soon enters the frame and seats herself slowly on Jeyopola's thigh, her sexy thighs exposed... Hahaha... Well Bhagath if you can actually pass such an enormous wind, then fine and welcome with me... Yes, at this point, he orders the defeated queen Yalaya to be brought in. The camera quickly moves backward and rises to eye level, when at the same time Himsha rises and stands aside. The camera pulls further back as Jeyopola strips himself violently and walks with his wobbly stomach and exposed genitals towards Yalaya. By the time he has reached her, the camera still on him, we can hear Yalaya's dress being torn apart. She lies naked on the floor. Now here is the tricky part. We only suggest that she is naked. And we don't explicitly show Jeyopola's genitals. Here, the camera quickly moves towards Jeyopola, yes as he nears her. The camera must lower itself to the worm's eye view again. And in that frame, a bare leg of Yalaya is visible and so is the naked Jeyopola whose wobbly giant stomach is covering his genitals. The camera moves backwards keeping Jeyopola in frame and the lying Yalaya in the right part of the frame. Her long hair is covering her nakedness. Here at this point, Jeyopola lowers himself to Yalaya as the camera rises to her sad face. Her body begins to rock back and forth. We can hear Jeyopola's moaning. In parallel, we hear Walika screaming in agony once again. All while the camera stays on Yalaya's face. She endures the defiling. Maybe after say about eight seconds, the camera rises to shoulder level by which time Jeyopola has risen and ordered his soldiers to take Yalaya away. Here the camera will approach Jeyopola in a close up as he walks towards his throne all sweating. The background is blurred all right. Now we hear Walika screaming out his dialogue in anger. The camera rushes to Walika who gets punched in the face by a soldier. And then the next second by Jeyopola's hand. But here, after the soldier has punched Walika the camera quickly turns to show Jeyopola who as we can understand is punching the air. When the camera turns towards Jeyopola, I want Birbal to move quickly to the spot marked on the floor. You have to lie down there. There will be fake blood and tiny fake pieces of scattered flesh on the floor. I said that when Jeyopola makes the punch the camera is on him. After the punch, keeping Jeyopola in the frame, the camera moves behind, reaching the dead Walika. The camera shows Walika lying in a pool of blood. Then, we can hear Jeyopola telling he needs a bath. Just then the camera rises to show queen Margafa in a close up. She is looking with a disinterested fashion towards the dead Walika. But then she looks up, towards the throne. Here, the camera quickly turns to show four semi-naked women walking away with Jeyopola, giggling. They simply enter and exit the frame. The camera continues moving to the throne where now Himsha sits herself leg upon leg on the throne, with jealousy teeming in her eyes. We end this single shot with the camera resting on Himsha's close-up."

Similar to the narration with the technicians, here too Jaseela just slam dunked onto the chair behind her. She was sweating profusely. Anju offered her a bottle of water. Jaseela smiled and took it. As she opened the bottle, claps erupted in the room. Jaseela started gulping the water with a contended face. Bhagath asked about the royal poet. Jaseela had dropped the poet from that scene and added him to the next.

CHAPTER XI

Cast

Back in Mumbai, Mohith came into the acting business primarily because he needed money to repay three loans. Because his father, the sole bread winner of the family, had to wrap up his tea shop due to lung cancer, Mohith had to stop going to college midway and desperately hunted for jobs. He even worked as a pet cleaner for three dogs of a Bollywood celebrity. The expenses for the dogs per month were way more than his salary. Still, Mohith endured. At nights, after gruelling work hours practically anywhere there was a job and money, Mohith would sit near the tattered steps leading to his small home that housed his parents and siblings, holding his favourite mirror he purchased when he was in the 6th standard. Mohith loved his face so much. The other day, while cutting a tile at a site, the blade flew off the cutter and slit his cheek. Mohith now looked like some medieval soldier carrying an injury he was proud of. His sun-tanned face gave the impression that he was well versed with life.

At the age of 28 with a receding hairline, no girlfriend, no job and no future, Mohith still felt confident. Someday he would make it big. He knew it. That was when Dr Putra the oncologist suggested Mohith try acting. There was a new television series looking for young energetic men. The series was to be shot in Kolaazham, the South Indian UT. Dr Putra's friend, one Dr Jasmine, had joined the crew as chief medical officer. Thus, on the Dr's suggestion and with money lent by him, Mohith left for Kolaazham. The audition went well. But a few women and some men too, told Mohith that he would get the role if he was willing to sleep with them. A terrified Mohith was seen crying one day at a bus stop, by Jaseela. On noticing that guy from the auditions, she enquired. She fired the women and men who 'offered' Mohith the role.

Jaseela loved the naivety displayed by Mohith. But she also knew being too innocent was not the formula to stay alive in that cut-throat industry. Her doubts were blown away the next instant when a pervert almost grabbed her butt as he passed by innocently. The pervert took Mohith to be a dumbass as well. But, like some superhero, it seemed Mohith calculated the pervert's move beforehand. And the next second, the pervert was crying at the top of his voice as Mohith held the twisted hand of the pervert firmly and tightly with a sort of lifeless expression that was equally menacing. Jaseela saw Jeyopola's merciless army general there. She introduced Mohith to Udit. Once, during the shoot of The Rhino Emperor's first season, several young women among the junior artists were swooning over the new heartthrob of tinsel town. Amidst the hectic schedule of the shoot, Jaseela even had a bet with Udit that Mohith would lose his virginity before the first season's shoot finished. Udit said that wouldn't happen. But as each episode of season one aired, Mohith went one step further from being just any actor to being a well sought after celebrity actor. And so, Jaseela prevailed.

Anju Leelavathi loved men. But she didn't like the concept of marriage and neither was she the flirtatious type. She loved children. But she didn't want to carry a baby in her stomach for nine months and then push the baby out and spend sleepless nights taking care of the baby. Anju was a selfish woman. She loved herself, her body and she loved the ten economically poor children she had decided to fund, for their education and wellbeing. On occasions, Anju enjoyed a man's warmth. But there were conditions. She didn't entertain drunkards or drug addicts. She didn't like teenagers. Either her age, 42, or in the thirties. Up to sixty was permissible. Beyond that, what if the guy gets a heart attack when he climaxes!!

Anju was not particularly interested in acting. But when Udit, her neighbour's son came one day with Wendy whom she didn't know then, she understood that here, playing a venomous king's jealous wife would fetch her more money and then maybe she would be able to start a school for the less fortunate children to study. She went full swing into her acting part full-fledged, when the entire team of season one of The Rhino Emperor pitched in money, a total of Rs 75 lakhs, for Anju to build her dream school. Anju cried like never before, that night. Udit and Jaseela even helped her to gain the permits to start the school building construction. It was on her property of 25 cents of land that the school was coming up. Anju was always thankful to Udit for spotting her acting talent.

Every day of the shoot she entered the set only after touching Jaseela's feet who placed her utmost trust upon this lady in her 40s to act out a pivotal role. And for a person who had never been in front of a movie camera in her life, Anju shined like a bright moonlight on set and in the hearts of the audience worldwide. Even Bhagath was full of praise for her acting prowess. Being the straightforward woman that Anju was, she liked Bhagath's quiet demeanour. In fact, she was waiting for their love making scene which was to come in the second season. Not that she was particularly interested in the scene, but she had a chance to challenge Bhagath face to face in acting. If her character was docile in the first season, she was turning rebellious in the second. And that love making scene was the start of that marked change.

It was the second time after they debuted together on screen eighteen years ago that the Birbal couple were uniting once again. Birbal as the defeated king and his cunning twin brother and Sharmeela as the defeated king's wife facing prison and torture under the tyrant Jeyopola's regime. When Sharmeela came to know that her character would be stripped naked and defiled by Jeyopola, she had her apprehensions. The demons from her personal life began surfacing, again. Birbal had to seek help from Jaseela, Udit and Bhagath regarding the matter. They all felt sorry for Sharmeela. Particularly Bhagath who had the added burden of having a young woman play his mistress, who also happened to share his elder daughter's name – Srividya. And then he himself had to strip his clothes and do a defiling act of a woman. The pressure was sky high for Birbal, Sharmeela and Bhagath. And being the single shot that Jaseela had envisioned, the torment only doubled or rather tripled.

In an unprecedented show of emotional maturity, it was Birbal's and Sharmeela's two teenage children who talked with their mother and convinced her that those demons would go away. They were there for her. After all, the defeated queen's predicament was only an act, a fake. Their mother could pull it off like no other. There, the family of four cried as a deeply troubled Jaseela felt relieved. She walked away from that scene, wiping her tears. She had seen several heart-warming moments in this hell of an industry called cinema. But this one, where the children took the reins for their parents, was going to stay in her mind till her death.

CHAPTER XII

Venkatesh

The calling bell rang. Amma opened the door. She smiled seeing Udit. "She is in the kitchen, son", said Amma. Udit smiled and went into the kitchen. He felt really surprised seeing Jaseela wear a nightie and perform the cooking.

"Have the children returned from school?", enquired Udit.

"No darling. They have that practice no", replied Jaseela. "Shall I make you some tea my love?"

"Ya one hot glass of tea would be nice. Have you written the list? I think we can take a taxi, get the kids and go to the grocery, a three-star dinner after that and return home. An evening to remember."

"You have to spend money when our monthly budget is so cramped darling?"

Udit looked at Jaseela. There was a comical feel to the scene. They laughed.

"Our lives in a parallel universe?", asked Jaseela.

"Nope. This universe. The only difference, you will be the worker. I will be the homemaker", responded Udit.

"Oho... Come here you sweety chweety cookie."

She beckoned Udit to her. Udit came to her and wrapped his hands around her stomach from behind. He smelled her sweaty neck. He kissed her neck.

"Any erotic feelings Udit?"

"Of course I do my dear. But I'll wait. Till our marriage is over."

"Oh you cliché middle class naïve Indian."

Jaseela turned her head and the couple kissed. Then she said, "Go talk to amma. I'll finish this, take a quick bath and we'll go ok?"

"As you say."

Udit kissed Jaseela's neck once again and went to the sitting room. In thirty minutes, the couple were out. Jaseela was driving. After a few minutes of silence, Jaseela said, "I feel something bad is about to happen Udit."

"You mean me happening to your life?"

"Not you, you asshole hahaha... Something else... You know about my sex sessions with Jonathan... His look that day, during the meeting with the execs... It was really menacing I must say. It was out of the blue."

Udit nodded.

"Now I have stopped that. Seems Wendy has begun dating him or something. I just can't understand that part."

"What part? Come on. Wendy is a human being. How long can she control her urges? Let her have fun I say. And simply forget about Jonathan's looks. Just drive now."

"Udit... I know that you know what I am saying."

"If whatever you have in mind transpires, let it be Jaseela. You can have the satisfaction that you created a cult classic series and that you gave so many people, including me, a steady income. We will love you for that."

"But my creation? Where did I go wrong Udit? Should I remain Jonathan's..."

Jaseela stopped the car and started to cry. Udit knew what was happening and probably what was going to happen. But he was not willing to give up. And he wasn't interested in seeing Jaseela cower at this point; not his ever-defiant Jaseela. In an unprecedented move he shouted, "I am not any spiritual master to guide you Jaseela. Right now, our focus is to meet with Venkatesh caterers. Let us do that first!! Now DRIVE!!"

Jaseela felt like being struck by lightning. But she needed that jolt; she needed Udit. At Venkatesh Caterers Jaseela and Udit waited with Smitha. Smitha knew the owner of this small catering unit. She had some family relation with the caterer. The trio had their doubts if this unit could actually cater to the food requirements of the massive Rhino unit. Venkatesh wanted to meet the director first. Only then would he sit with the finance managers and discuss the rates. Jaseela was already out of those weak sentimental thoughts thanks to Udit. Now all she had in mind was the rehearsal of the single shot to be performed in exactly two weeks' time. All the agreements had been signed.

Soon other thoughts crept in. In a disgraceful move meant for Jaseela, some of the crew members who had asked Mohith to sleep with them in season one, had been reinstated. And in season two, the celebrity Mohith had a slight fall out with Jaseela on that matter because Mohith had actually begun to sleep with one of those women now, Supriya. Being a friend that she thought he was, Jaseela was totally shocked to witness Mohith's arrogant transformation. That would mean she was no longer the person who could keep people under control. Jaseela's superiority would be questioned. Yet, she was forced to play along as the stakes were at the highest level; she couldn't replace Mohith or even kill off that famous character he was playing, yet. And that was just the tip of the iceberg.

Jaseela even began to have doubts about her most trusted cast and crew. Who was loyal to her and who was not? She even had doubts about Udit... Why wasn't he interested in having sex with her? Didn't he love her? Was he feeling a disgust for a woman who slept with many men before? Was Udit having sex with someone else? Jaseela!! She was shaken from her train of thoughts when Udit shook her shoulder. Venkatesh was sitting in front of them. He was in his seventies. He had no teeth in the front. He was chewing pan. He looked jovial.

"So, you want me to cook for you? How many days will that be? 45 days? Your crew number will be 150, I guess. I once did cook for a Tamil film back in 1992. 42 days my team and I toiled. In the end, no money. Seems the producer's money drained away."

Udit, Jaseela and Smitha now knew that Venkatesh had actually no idea what he was dealing with. Smitha came forward and began to explain, "Chittappa, you see we are part of a television series..."

"Serial? All illicit affairs and pregnancies", interrupted Venkatesh, scoffing.

"This is not like those Chittappa. The series is a big thing. It's the talk of the town, among the youth and film fanatics", said Smitha.

"I see. Can I get a role in this series?", mocked Venkatesh.

That mocking went straight into the hearts of the trio who were already wasting their most precious time here when they had lots to do at the set. This was Tim's job actually. Jaseela kept quiet. Udit feigned an incoming phone call and left the room. Smitha didn't give up fast. She took out her phone, opened the gallery and gave the phone to Venkatesh saying, "See for yourself what we are about to do." The old droopy eyes of Venkatesh began to brighten and then turned into ultra peak surprise level. The massive sets, the arrangements made... the businessman in him suddenly saw insane amounts of money and immense fame if he employed his culinary skills for this massive project. And then came the selfies with several celebrities... His mouth opened wide when he saw Smitha's selfie with Bhagath Lavanya Shekhar. "Bhagath Lavanya Shekhar", said a breathless Venkatesh as he raised his head and bulging eyes, towards Smitha. There was an 'agreed' written on Venkatesh's face.

CHAPTER XIII

Planner

Jonathan kissed Jaseela on her cheeks. He had a wild urge to have a rocking session with her. But then he contained himself. Jonathan could see anger fuming in Jaseela's entire body. He knew it was about the scene he made during the screening of that war sequence. The need to disrupt Jaseela's work was the only thing going on in Jonathan's mind that day. And that day went like Jonathan planned. Now, he was in the meeting with Jaseela and the crew before the trial shoot planned to happen four days later. As for his sexual urges, he had Wendy and a few junior artists to quench his thirst. He had placed Heyson at the correct spot. He had reinstated Kannaki, Supriya and Das, the three people who had been fired by Jaseela. Kannaki was excellent in bed. Jonathan had to spend more money on this gang to jump to his side despite their ill feelings for Jaseela.

Jonathan had ill feelings towards Udit. He could see the strong romance transmitting between Jaseela and Udit. Jonathan stayed in place; his feelings put in shackles. Time and patience would be rewarded. Now that all were in the perfect place, Jonathan could just sit aside and watch Jaseela's world crumble. She would fall down one day miserably and break her soul. This unprofessional piece of shit. She had the audacity to insult Jonathan, the money giver, the lifeline of this major television series. And she did what she did. As for Jaseela, she wanted to slap Jonathan a hundred times on his face for insulting her with the reinstatement of three vile people. And the war sequence debacle... Jaseela kept her feelings in check.

Udit was in Jonathan's mind. He knew about Udit's passion for cinema and Jaseela. Here was this incorruptible personality. Udit was a bane for the film industry. No. He was not naïve. He simply built a fortress around him, an impregnable fortress which only few people could get through. Jonathan needed to break into that fortress. With only four days left for the trial take of the single duration shot, Jonathan knew that that fortress had to be demolished soon.

He was going to London for a few days. He wanted to be with his children. Constant sex with several women with different tastes was actually making Jonathan bored of the very thought. He wanted to spend time with his children. He wanted to unwind. He wanted to take care of his children, be the father that he often escaped from becoming. Maybe he would take his children for a picnic. They could take a camper van and drive around the whole UK; maybe spillover to the whole of Europe. Maybe Jonathan will ask Elsa to join. Maybe they could come to terms with each other and move on, for the kids' sake. Jonathan missed his long dead parents. He missed his own fatherhood... He was kind of wanting a break from all this negativity. He even felt remorse. Just because Jaseela told her lover first about the single shot, why was that an insult for Jonathan? If he had a check on his ego that day, today he would still be having a roller coaster ride with Jaseela; she wouldn't mind. All that blew with the wind. Now the key had turned.

There was no turning back. Tim asked if Jonathan would lose any money once the series removed Jaseela and put Wendy as the writer/director, after all this investment. "I can't take my father in law's fortunes to the grave, can I?", was the answer. But Jonathan knew Tim knew that most of the money invested here was from the massive profit Little Further Up earned from the first season's airing. Almost 70% invested here for the second season was from the profits. And only Tim knew that. Tim made sure the government officials here were fed with enough money to keep the books 'neat and clean'. Tim was the only person Jonathan trusted at this moment.

Even as Jonathan sat with Jaseela and the other crew members and talked about the project for about an hour in his office room, these were the thoughts that rummaged through his mind. He hugged Jaseela and wished her the best for the trial shoot. There was a part in him that loved Jaseela, a part in him that didn't want to leave. Jonathan felt he would never see Jaseela ever again, a premonition. He wanted to stand on a stage and spit out a twenty-page soliloquy that effectively showed how dirty-minded he was, how he wished to be a good human, how much he detested life... Brushing those idiotic thoughts away, the no-surprise theatre prodigy left for the airport once the meeting wrapped up.

CHAPTER XIV

Tim

Tim was a happy man for two weeks. His boss had left for London. He could have Wendy all to himself. She too preferred Tim. He was soft towards Wendy. He had begun to have feelings for her. He loved her children. The kids had begun to like him. And though his sex with Wendy was not wrong, he always felt he was deceiving Jonathan in some manner. He was the only person who was kept in the loop regarding Jonathan's plans. Jonathan wanted Wendy to replace Jaseela. He wanted the show to go forward. But Jaseela had to be removed. The single long duration shot idea had to be scrapped.

Tim was given the charge of the entire production until Jonathan returned. He had to oversee the trial taking place in four days' time and Jaseela's eventual destruction to follow. Somewhere inside, Tim knew all this was wrong. To sabotage the dreams of a woman, of an entire team. He had deep respect for Jaseela. Tim knew only Jaseela had that mettle to envision and pull off that gigantic single shot. But he had to live as well. He had to bring in some miscreants for the trial shoot. Through Wendy, he had given specific instructions to those jobless drunks. They would be arrested. But they would be taken out soon. How low Tim had stooped to, coming to this project. It was Tim with Wendy's help who planned the attack on Roopa's studio. And now the miscreants. He just wanted to escape. He had wanted to tell Wendy to call off the attack on Roopa's studio. He called off the miscreant plan for the trial shoot, at the last minute.

Tim and his team already had a gargantuan amount of paperwork regarding the finances to be done. And he was assigned the psychological warfare to destroy Jaseela as well. Tim became too tired. He loved the accounting part, he loved Wendy. But becoming something like a warlord was not his thing. As he kissed Wendy passionately, he said, "Why don't we quit Wendy? I can take you and the kids to the UK. We can start afresh." After the session, Wendy lay down panting with Tim's head on her stomach. Caressing his hair she said, "I know where this whole thing is going Tim. But I can't leave just like that. I deceived Jaseela. I have to make amends with her. I love you. But I won't ask you to stay. Just know that I am carrying your baby."

Tim raised his head and swirled his body counter clockwise and the next second his face was close to hers. They looked deeply into each other.

"Are you sure about...?"

"I am sure it's yours. With Jon there was protection. Always."

"Darling... Are you sure about what you told me a second ago?"

Wendy smiled. A shyness enveloped her out of nowhere. Tim just saw a dream where he and Wendy got married in the royal hall set the next day. In that dream Jonathan was clapping happily for Tim. In reality, Tim knew his comradeship with Jonathan had ended.

CHAPTER XV

Jeyopola's stomach

Only four days were left for the trial shoot of the single duration shot. And less than a month or so only for the main shoot. Smitha had to make around 200 severed heads, the same number of hands and legs as well. This season had more wars and gore. The violence would escalate. And Smitha with her team, began to work on the mammoth effort with more zest and zeal. Even her husband came in to help her out. Her department was one of the most visited, by the media and general public as well. Jaseela had decided to open the film set to an exclusive 200 winners of a raffle draw to promote the second season of The Rhino Emperor. And every time someone came to Smitha's station, her work would get stalled for at least 10 minutes. Her husband came in handy.

Bhagath tried the prosthetic wobbly stomach. This was the moment Smitha had been waiting for, for the last one year. One man whom Smitha deeply admired was right in front of her wearing a stomach she made. The wobbly stomach was latched onto Bhagath. And he felt the weight almost immediately. The 8 Kg was beginning to put pressure on Bhagath's back. And the wobbliness was actually making Bhagath's walking pretty difficult. The stomach simply wouldn't orient itself. And Bhagath would involuntarily try to control the stomach with his hands. Jaseela arrived to see the prosthetic and how Bhagath was managing. She had just come back from the screening of the war scene that would be followed by the single long duration shot that would air as S02E01. Jaseela was in a bad mood. She didn't want to think about that screening whatsoever. She didn't want that negativity to seep into the minds of her cast and crew. Sitting inside her car at the parking lot, Jaseela took a deep breath. She wanted Udit's kiss, but he was in Mumbai with Heyson to get some special gear for the cameras. She wanted to cry. But, Jaseela fixed a confident air onto her demeanour, passed wind and walked to Smitha's station. Jaseela liked the action of Bhagath trying to control his wobbly stomach. "We will use this, Bhagath. You are a genius", commented Jaseela. Smitha looked enquiringly at Jaseela who went to her immediately and hugged her saying, "You are doing the worst job among us all. Making bloodied severed hands and legs... I love you for that."

There was a laugh in the department. As Bhagath got off the stomach he commented, "It is kind of hurting my back. Can the weight be reduced, Smitha? I mean you can make it look weighty right but not actually heavy." "Bhagath the materials used are like that. Wait, we will try to lend more support to your back with extra latches that can go between your legs. You know, distribute the tension." "I am already tensed about meeting Lucky Rajput with this stomach of yours. And here he comes". Lucky Singh Rajput and Smitha worked out a quick redesign of the stomach with extra latches for even distribution of weight and tension.

In just half an hour, Smitha made Bhagath wear the better equipped stomach. Now, this was more comfortable, more agile. Even the sword fighting sessions felt easier than expected despite the wobbliness. Smitha's husband brought her a cup of coffee for her to take a break as they saw Bhagath behave like a child shaking and dancing with his wobbly prosthetic bulging stomach.

CHAPTER XVI

War

Because the first season of the colossal tv series The Rhino Emperor was an unprecedented success, Jaseela wanted the second season's first episode to begin with an equally colossal bang. And so the war sequence that was actually written for the end of season one, became season two's start. And Mitra Saha the editor sat in her Chennai studio for a whole month to bring to life Jaseela's maverick vision of the whopping 25-minute duration action packed war scene between Jeyopola and Walika in which Walika eventually concedes defeat. The shoot of the war scene itself was a tumultuous affair with the need to hire around 270 men, 100 horses, 25 elephants and to keep them fit and fed for 26 days, the number of days that was needed to complete the scene. All the members of the cast and crew got to see how crazy Jaseela could get to get what she wanted on screen. If the onscreen war was breaking the nerves of the two kings, the offscreen war to pull off such a behemoth of a human endeavour was as much punishing. That scene alone cost Rs 4 Cr to make.

Mitra had lost weight due to the pressure in speeding up the editing. She had to sit through late nights to reach the new deadline pushed forward by the execs at Little Further Up. The execs were pushed by Jonathan who decided to take a break from the job and go to London, to his children. So he decided he wanted to watch the completed war scene before the month end. Actually, the finished war scene was not due until the middle of the next month. But, Jonathan wanted to crush Jaseela. And one way was to put pressure on the editing of that one pivotal war scene that was of paramount importance in adding that much favoured flavour to the series. That push didn't sit well with Jaseela, but she didn't want to start a verbal war with Jonathan, lest that lessen the morale of the crew and cast. Jaseela didn't know why Jonathan was showering this level of animosity upon her. Was it because she stopped having sex with him? Was Jonathan such a lowlife?

Mitra had to re-arrange her entire life, literally, to speed-up the editing of the war scene. She in fact shifted to her studio for almost ten days to save time on transportation. She couldn't even call her children or husband during those days as she was neck-deep in cutting and pasting the shots. To make matters worse, Jonathan made sure Jaseela wasn't there to soothe Mitra's hectic schedule. Jonathan wanted to see the updates of the works done by every other department on a regular basis, overseen by Jaseela personally which meant Jaseela got to see the final output of the war scene only on the day of screening along with Jonathan, the execs and the OTT officials who were going to buy The Rhino Emperor. For the mixing of the sound tracks, Jonathan sent Wendy to Devaprasad Rai's studio. Wendy made Rai do the tracks her way, completely ignoring Jaseela's inputs. Jaseela thus got stuck in the film set. Mitra got stuck in her studio.

On the day of the screening, Jonathan made Wendy contact a few online media channels to come and capture the reactions of the execs, select cast and crew. Jaseela could sit through for about ten minutes only, of the war. This was not her war scene. This was not what she had envisioned. Mitra was not to blame. She did what she could do. Jaseela wanted to strangle Jonathan and Wendy. She wanted to set that screen on fire. Jaseela wanted to walk out of the screening room. But outside, the online media channels were prowling around to capture and create gossip. And she would walk straight into their gaping mouths if she left now. So Jaseela simply had to clench her fists and sit through the total 25 gruelling minutes of the war scene with a level of insult and pain never experienced before. She wanted to cry on Udit's shoulders, have a soothing kiss from him... But he was sent to Mumbai with Heyson. As the war scene was about to finish, with Walika about to lay down his crown, a visibly angry yet tired Jaseela walked towards where Jonathan was sitting. She sat next to him. Walika had laid down his crown now. Looking at Jonathan, Jaseela enquired flatly, "Should I have sex with you again to stop this torment?"

Jeyopola took the crown and with a smirk mixed with a mocking expression he raised the crown slowly, towards the top of his head. But like a sudden reflex, Jeyopola threw away that golden crown. Jonathan looked at Jaseela. There was a menacing look twinkling in his eyes in that dark screening room visible only to Jaseela. "I really want to have sex with you Jaseela... A long duration sex... But you see Jaseela, you won't be in the moment during that sex like you used to. You will do it out of spite. I hate spite. I hate surprises. You have Udit now. I have... I can't remember how many there are, you know, women... Good luck with the trial shot darling. Now come. We need to talk business with those OTT fellows." Jonathan kissed Jaseela on her cheeks. The lights came on just then. Everyone, including Jaseela got up and clapped their hands in excitement, in satisfaction. Jaseela was burning within. She saw Mitra leave the room in tears.

CHAPTER XVII

Kannaki

Kannaki was sold to a drug lord while a child, in the outskirts of Bangalore. As she reached puberty, she was pushed into prostitution. Of the many men who had their fill with her body, one was an assistant director who eventually brought Kannaki her first film assignment. She was his assistant. In the mornings she helped with the shoot in her limited ways. In the night, every night, she had to assist the director, the producer or the cameraman. The assistant director got paid for this arrangement. She got 30% of what he got. And so as time passed, Kannaki crossed ten years in the film field. And she was a prominent make-up artist now. And a sexaholic. Her body wanted sex. Her mind wanted to wander the Himalayas. But there too, she would have to sell her body she knew. Kannaki despised her life.

When she saw Mohith during the preproduction of the first season, it was just the usual question for her. A crucial question for the listener though. Many young male stars got their stars changed when they shared the bed with Kannaki. She saw no sin in that. She was asking them. They were not after her. Kannaki didn't care when she was ousted from Jaseela's set. Jaseela already had some international fellow to beautify the main leads. All Kannaki got was to make the soldiers look bloodied. She got bored easily. But she didn't forget Mohith. Life had taught Kannaki to be tough and imposing. No one showed her any leniency in her growing years. Now she would show none.

The first thing Kannaki did when Jonathan took her back in, was to go to Mohith and slap his face and kick his genitals. In less than a month after the first season aired, Mohith had changed into a top-notch celebrity. And so with the onset of the second season, Kannaki didn't see the retaliation coming. Mohith kissed her violently and they toppled onto the bed and tore the bed into pieces amidst the wildest sex they both had in recent times. The moaning and screaming were outright disgusting. Sparks of an uncontrollable fiery wrath kept flying off their sweaty bodies. As Kannaki got up after the session, she slapped Mohith and left the room. There was anger brimming in her. She wanted Mohith to cower under her presence. She wanted to trample him. She hated him. She vowed to destroy him.

The next day as Kannaki cleaned herself and presented herself to Jonathan to thank him for taking her back in, there too, she had to undress. Kannaki just wanted to end her life. But the clever guy Jonathan was, he seduced her making her feel like a woman. And for the first time in her life, Kannaki felt like a normal woman. Jonathan treated her well. He didn't spring onto her body. In fact, they just talked for the whole day in that luxury apartment of Jonathan's. Jonathan knew Wendy would slip away soon. He had his doubts about everyone. He had no doubts about Kannaki. She was to take over Tim's job once Jonathan returned from the UK in two weeks' time. Kannaki knew Tim would move out soon. By then, she had enough time to sew threads of discord in the set. And Mohith was her hot target; that naïve celebrity bastard.

CHAPTER XVIII

Wendy

Wendy initially felt a solace lost a long time ago, falling into her life back again when she began seeing Jonathan. It didn't take long for her to realise she was just one among many women in Jonathan's life. That was when Tim stepped in. Ironically, when Wendy thought she was caught in the drifts of the windy thing called existence, Tim offered her a new life. He knew about Jonathan using Wendy's body for sex. He couldn't stop Jonathan yet. But Wendy knew and became more confident whenever Tim diverted Jonathan to other women sparing Wendy.

Wendy was an ambitious woman. She did in fact direct one episode of the first season. But she wanted more. She wanted to be the writer/director of the whole second and the third season of The Rhino Emperor. Jaseela had discussed her ideas with Wendy. Not that Wendy wanted to oust Jaseela off the project. She could stay as one of the writers. Wendy would take over the megaphone. Her jealous notions and dream-world building came to a standstill when she realised she was pregnant with Tim's child. Wendy knew Tim would be excited. He adored her two children. And now his child was coming.

Though Wendy was excited as well, she didn't want the child. Wendy didn't want to stay away from the production for nine months. She was not ready to take care of another baby for a whole year and then return to her job. Wendy entered a great dilemma. There was Jaseela who was craving to be a mother. Here was Wendy herself with child, locked for life. Should she destroy the child? She wanted a better life for her children and herself. Tim was the answer. She would have to feign happiness and give Tim his child. But could she do it?

Suddenly Wendy's days with Jaseela flooded her mind. Days well spent in the film institute. Both the women got first-hand experience to be free from home. They would often roam around the city, take trains to nearby villages, sit at beaches wearing shorts and armless t-shirts commenting and giggling at the men who passed them by with drooling mouths. Wendy and Jaseela too would drool over men. Not men who wanted to look cool. But men who went about their daily lives, who had hidden personas in them. Wendy was quick to grasp such men. She would look at the old man selling peanuts on the beach and tell Jaseela he looked like Dostoevsky, the ever-brooding human.

The duo especially found it interesting to pry upon married men and how the fathers looked after their children in the public. Many were the dictatorial type. Some encouraged their children. Most were sceptical, often claiming the children were losers. Once one such father's elbow touched Wendy's bosom accidently. It was an accident. But the way he kept on saying sorry to Wendy made her feel sorry for him. One thing led to the other, and Wendy had her second sexual encounter. It was mutual. But then remorse struck that father and Wendy. He was the bookshop owner near the film institute. Wendy cried that night. Jaseela was there to help her get through that sickening remorse.

All those years later, Wendy needed Jaseela's counsel badly now. But how would Jaseela react to Wendy, that too at this point? Jaseela probably knew about Wendy's history with Jonathan. Jaseela's was pure creative energy that she released while she slept with Jonathan. Wendy saw opportunity. She hated herself for deceiving Jaseela who took her under her wings. Even now, Jaseela showed genuine love and care despite knowing Wendy's doings. Wendy cursed herself for being an asshole, for being a woman, for being an opportunist, for allowing Tim to transfer a child into her womb...

All that anger and confusion just flew off the window when she saw that look in Tim's eyes. She felt shy. Wendy felt shy, probably after ten years or so. An epiphany occurred to her. The Rhino Emperor was not her calling. She already had treatments of ideas for two or three series written. She should pursue those. Her own ideas. Tim's excited look said it all. He would be there for her. Through every turbulent tide and wind... They decided to quit from the show.

CHAPTER XIX

Heyson

Heyson Prasanna had just come back to the film set after signing the documents of a lush farming land in a remote village in Tamil Nadu. His team of assistants had already finished installing two poles and cables that ran the length of the set, a total of 1.6 kilometres. The camera would be mounted to a rig screwed to a plate fixed with rollers on the cable for the high-rise shots. The cable had to be pulled down for the camera operator to fix it onto his torso for the eye level shots and the floor level shots. Heyson showed immense interest in the planning stage of the single shot despite his allegiance to Jonathan. That was in fact a perfect cover thought Jonathan, before he got the perfect opportunity to blow Jaseela off course in the coming days.

Heyson knew deep down he was doing a totally unethical thing. He was proud to work with a talent like Jaseela but saddened at his flexible spine's miserable stooping towards money put forth by Jonathan. Another more troubling moment was about to shake Heyson to the core. Just before the trial shoot that early morning was about to commence, as he stood near the tenth elephant upon which Bhagath had seated himself for a practice, Heyson helped Srividya mount the elephant. As she availed Heyson's help, she whispered, "I missed my period, Heyson."

He caught her eyes for a micro-second. They were welled up with tears. Heyson was shocked. He had noticed Srividya even before the photoshoot. And he felt blown away seeing her dark skin tone. She felt like a goddess to Heyson. He did try a few times to hit it off with her, but Mohith had won her heart. But human jealousy had its ways. Jonathan's offer to Heyson was he would be the in-house D.O.P for all the future projects of Little Further Up. That meant Heyson would have a stable salary, better prospects. That very thought and his closeness to the fund provider had made Heyson a powerful sort of guy in Jaseela's set. Heyson found ways to intimidate the women. He talked dirty to Smitha and Anju. Almost all the women in the camp hated Heyson. Kannaki and Supriya were his companions. And it was Supriya under Kannaki's guidance who cajoled Srividya into Heyson's room. She just had to sleep with him. And her future was secure.

The beginner that Srividya was, and her recent fall out with Mohith made her Heyson's target. It was his first time with a young actor. It was just twenty days ago. After the successful trial shoot, Heyson ran to the toilet. He released all the puke built up in his stomach. He got severe diarrhoea. Heyson felt fear like never before. He felt weak. He felt all the money he possessed was just a waste of paper. He couldn't breathe. Heyson shivered like a leaf caught in a storm. What would he tell to his parents when they came to know? What would his would-be think? He fainted in the toilet. It took almost four hours for someone to hunt down Heyson. He had a high temperature. He was rushed to the medical officer stationed in the set. But he went to see Kannaki immediately.

CHAPTER XX

Anger

Bhagath and his wife Soumya were sitting on the floor at 4:30 AM doing their daily meditation when Bhagath felt something uneasy. The day of the trial shoot of the single shot had arrived. Bhagath had to be on set by 5:40 AM in make-up and costume. And Bhagath knew something or someone had just arrived to spoil his day. He got up troubled and mumbling slur words to himself. Soumya heard those words. Worried, she too rose from the floor. As they ventured into the sitting room, they noticed the entrance door open. And they also noticed Lavanya Shekhar, sitting on the sofa. Lavanya was tired.

Anger began to boil within Bhagath the instant he saw his mother. Of all the days, that lady had to appear in front of him on this critical one. Knowing her son's disdain for her, Lavanya said she was brought in by a guy called Tim upon Jaseela's order to give Bhagath a surprise on his birthday. That critical day was Bhagath's birthday. Bhagath said nothing. He left for the set in the pajamas he was wearing. Soumya stood there breathing heavily. She saw hatred harboured in her mother-in-law's face and body. She too left the house. Lavanya sat there, all alone, knowing well why her son despised her. Lavanya was too old. Or else she would have run to her son and fallen onto his feet. All she could do now was weep. Sridhanya came with a cup of hot tea for her grandmother.

Bhagath had burst out in anger at Jaseela for insulting him with his mother's presence, in front of the whole cast as Jaseela was about to give them a final brush up, in the royal hall set. This happened just before the trial shoot was about to begin. Anju, figuring out what had happened, quickly took Bhagath to the side and explained the situation. Bhagath now decided to wait for Jonathan. He would tear out the head of Jonathan. Jaseela sat on her seat, dejected, tired. Bhagath came to her. He apologised profusely. He even went as far as touching Jaseela's feet for forgiveness. She simply cried. Bhagath sat next to Jaseela and caressed her hair like he would to his daughters. Jaseela felt that protective shield return, one that had gone when her father had died two years ago. "Forgive this old man my child", begged Bhagath. For some reason Bhagath was beginning to get very angry those days.

Now as Bhagath donned his costume along with the prosthetic stomach and went to act his part, his mind was filled with memories of his childhood. Never once did he smile at his parents. No matter the gifts he got, the opulence he grew in, the education he received, the stardom he acquired... his sister's hatred for him... Bhagath's father had been bedridden for years now. His mother had gone through much hardship. There were financially tough times. Now like his father, his mother too had reached the end of her life. Maybe, fate needed Bhagath to reconcile with his parents first. And then, maybe then, he would face his sister. After the successful trial, Bhagath and Soumya went to their hut. But not before celebrating the success of the trial shot and the whole crew and cast singing Bhagath the happy birthday song in the royal hall.

CHAPTER XXI

Phobia

After Jaseela and Udit kissed with true passion, she said, "I want to do it with you Udit. My body really aches for you". Jaseela kissed Udit again. Udit's mother's voice once again reiterated that dinner was ready. To Jaseela he said, "Not yet my love. Come."

Udit was cherophobic. He never had a good, decent childhood. It was always sickness and poverty. When his father deserted the family, that was when Udit realised there was never going to be any happiness, in any amount whatsoever, to ever grace Udit. And after all those years of having lived a harsh life, Udit did put up a brave face. But deep within he was living in a hurricane. That hurricane was constantly devouring him. He never had long lasting friends. He would always see his mother come from work crying. When Udit got selected to Pune film institute, the only thing his mother said was to never destroy a woman's body who came to him for a chance in a film. Udit saw years of defilement in his mother's eyes.

Jaseela was a revolution and a revelation to Udit. She was more than everything he had thought about what any living human could be. She was a great friend, a great teacher, a great lover, a great parent... When they first met in the institute campus, Udit hadn't eaten for three days. He had no money and no guts to ask anyone for money. When he was introduced to Jaseela, she saw hunger boiling in those innocent eyes. The first thing she did right then was drag him to the campus canteen. No one had touched him in that manner. It was as though she owned him. She had in fact. Jaseela loved him. Each time Jaseela was eager about sleeping with Udit, he brushed that notion away because he somehow felt that that would be the end of their thing. Udit was scared. He was cherophobic.

When Jaseela and Udit returned to Jaseela's hut from the mess hall after dinner, she started voicing her doubts and concerns about the very existence of the second season. Even during the dinner, her mind was filled with the war scene screening fiasco. In the hut, Jaseela frankly spoke to Udit about the people who were playing double standards with her. Only Devaprasad Rai, Bhagath and Smitha didn't figure in that list.

"How come I don't figure in that list Jaseela?", enquired a slightly irked Udit though he put up a smile.

"Udit... It's my helpless mind. My period has begun. It's feeling painful. Tomorrow's trial shoot. The pressure... My mind is not here my love...", replied Jaseela almost panting. She sat on a chair grabbing a water bottle. The cherophobic Udit couldn't contain himself.

"So, you have doubts about my loyalty to you Jaseela? I mean what do you want really? From your friends or me? Should we be loyal to you? Can't I love you?", asked Udit as the spit that formed in his mouth got stuck in his throat. He choked. Why did this have to end so soon, thought Udit with a dagger piercing his heart.

"Udit... I didn't mean to hurt you. I don't know what I'm thinking or doing. It's my situation. It's all going haywire..."

"What's going haywire!!"

Throwing the bottle down and rising abruptly with anger flashing in her eyes Jaseela yelled out, "Me! Damn it! ME JASEELA AKBAR!! I am failing here can't you see Udit? Well how can you? You have built a strong wall all around you to protect yourself from possible downfalls.

That's what makes you a failure Udit. You never try. You simply tag along. You don't want to make attempts, take risks. Oh ya that life shattering meeting with my cousin and that other bumb at the Equator Hotel. Boohoohoo. Keep crying kid! That's life. You were never the fighter Udit. But I am!! Remember the first time we met at the institute? Remember how I dragged you to the canteen? That's power Udit. Dynamics. Seizing the moment. And now what are we? What are we? Take us for example." Interrupting her Udit retorted,

"Ya what about us? What should I have seized Jaseela?? Your body? Do you think having sex is the basic benchmark for knowing if a person is a fighter? If that relation will last? Why should I boast around about my battles with life to everyone? That's my thing! I am the silent contributor. And... Is that what this drama is about? Will your agony stop if I have sex with you??"

Udit had blurted out the exact question Jaseela asked Jonathan during the war scene's screening. Jaseela felt aghast. Was her mind always nagging her to have sex with Udit simply to know if he was loyal to her??

And before Jaseela could move a muscle, Udit was out. He left the set. He walked away partially hiding the tears. There was agony as that is part of every breakup. But Udit felt sort of happy as well. From the start, Udit knew he wasn't destined to be with Jaseela, that monumental human. There was a part in him that always kept a distance from the woman he loved deeply. Udit wanted to walk back to Jaseela. He wanted to kiss her. He wanted to witness that legendary single long duration trial shot. He wanted to experience those goosebumps. But he just left. Udit felt deceived, belittled. Years later, Udit would use the word 'escape' to sum up that act, that walk-out he did, during one of Jaseela's life's most critical times.

CHAPTER XXII

Message

Srividya was an emotionally matured woman. Though an orphan, Srividya knew the trials and tribulations a woman would have to face in the entertainment industry. Jaseela or Udit or Anju wouldn't always be there to protect her. After she had sex with Mohith, almost three days after she joined the camp, Srividya was on cloud nine. Mohith was highly creative in bed. And Srividya got a good amount of money as advance. She got to hone her acting skills in the workshops. Life was good. She got to know Bhagath better. He was like a father figure. It was difficult for them both to feel like the characters in one moment and be a dad and daughter like, later on. On her advice, Bhagath asked his own daughter Srividya to be there during the workshops. Things went better at work.

Srividya began to have an active sex life. But soon the celebrity Mohith began to go after the junior artists. There was Supriya and Das to thank for. It was then that Srividya noticed Heyson. Kannaki had set them up. Heyson was a rough guy. But, when he began to confess about his allegiance to Jonathan and how that was affecting his morale, Srividya saw a human in him. She felt she needed to do something to make him get better. It was more like a respect for Jaseela that Srividya took it upon herself to better the mind of Heyson.

The human in Heyson immediately turned into a monster in bed. And Srividya loved every second of it. She even made sure no one except Kannaki know of her escapades with Heyson. Those were happy days. Anju had her doubts though. She would often confront Srividya like a guardian. But the young woman simply brushed her away. Life was good. Until she missed her period. Just eight days before the trial shoot of the single shot, Srividya's period was supposed to start. She never had delays. She mentioned the missing period to Heyson as he helped her up the tenth elephant. Even Bhagath enquired about the emotional dryness on her face. But she said nothing to Bhagath.

Srividya knew she had to endure the trial no matter what. She was given a new life by Jaseela and Wendy. Maybe the tension and pressure of that shot was doing tricks to her menstrual cycle. Srividya, along with the others, went through a perfect shot trial. It was so perfect, Jaseela was ecstatic despite her alleged break up with Udit, felt Srividya. She did notice that Heyson was absent from the set. The celebration and birthday bash in the royal hall rocked.

As she sat at a corner of the set sipping coffee along with Anju and Smitha, the tea glass slipped from her hand and Srividya fell backward. She was unconscious. A tensed Bhagath and Kumar carried Srividya to the medical officer. The doctor examined her. She came out tensed and told to no one in particular, "Get Jaseela here quickly!!"

CHAPTER XXIII

Trial shoot

Jaseela felt an ominous foreboding when her voice cracked over the megaphone. All who assembled at the set for the trial shoot of the crucial single shot stood confused. Was Jaseela crying? Where was Udit? But before anyone could ask about their doubts to anyone, Jaseela's firm and defiant voice sprang to the air through the megaphone: Action!! That was assurance enough for that congregation to get into action. All the lead actors, all the junior artists, all the crew were all on their toes, were holding their breaths, were giving their best, their hundred percent to make the trial shot itself a legendary cinematic moment to talk about in the years to come.

Every second of the shot was crucial. Every movement of the camera had to be precise. Every actor had to play their assigned part as well as they could. For a total of 25 minutes that the shot lasted, it would be fair to say no one breathed an ounce of oxygen. The whole cast and crew held their breaths. The camera had travelled through every nook and corner of the giant set by then, manoeuvred by Heyson's team. And as the camera, held by a sweating Heyson now, finally focussed a close-up onto the semi naked Himsha the seductress, Srividya sat on the throne looking with boiling jealousy towards Anju's Margafa. Jaseela who was holding a handheld monitor and moving with the camera throughout the entire take, now yelled: Cut!!

Everyone hugged the nearest person there was, in excitement. Heyson left the royal hall almost immediately.

Incidentally, there was no one near Jaseela. Her eyes did hunt for Udit for a second. And then she realised he had left. Because of her. Udit couldn't be a part of this shot, this critical shot, because she had accused him of cheating her. But did she say that? As the success of the trial shot was still raving in the royal hall along with Bhagath's birthday bash, Jaseela escaped from the hall. She walked out not knowing where to go. Somehow, she finally ended up in the canteen. Just as she sat down, Venkatesh came up to her with a hot cup of chocolate milk and some biscuits he made. Amid the tears Jaseela smiled at Venkatesh and took a sip of the drink. It was really good. Venkatesh sat next to her. They had become good friends in a short time.

"I saw him walk away madam at around 11 PM yesterday."

"You can call me Jaseela, Venki anna."

"Ok... I saw him walk away at 11 PM yesterday, Jaseela."

Teary eyed, Jaseela giggled still. Venkatesh's humour was good.

"Did you get your selfie with Bhagath, Venki anna?"

"No dear... I did go and introduce myself. Seems he had eaten from the hotel that I owned some forty years back. Seems he still remembers the vada I made! The chutney too. Why do I need a selfie then??"

Jaseela wiped her tears, impressed with what Venkatesh was saying.

"Are you going to make that same vada for him today evening?"

"Not just for him my dear but for you and all of the humans in this set. Almost 1400 vadas for 700 members. My people are already into it as we speak."

"1398 vadas anna. Two vadas won't be eaten. He is not here."

"I don't care. How can I make only 1398 vadas? If there are more, we can all share. Less is the problem."

"I just said."

"My child, I would prefer to make 1400 vadas. I want to cook for *all* the 700 members of this family, be they good or bad. No one is perfect. Even this skeleton of a man you call anna, has a very dark past. I am trying to make it better, even today, in this age... You can have doubts, raise them, but clear them... I don't believe in the idea that you only have one life so travel and eat and enjoy life. My idea is even if you are stuck in one place for the rest of your life, pray that you can stay there with a person or group of people you can be with, you know you can suffer with..."

"I am alone anna... You know who my role model is? My twin sister Jameela. She has three beautiful children. I want children. I want to work and take care of my children... Ha ha, Udit says he will stay home and look after the kids. I can be the breadwinner."

"That thought is an ever-increasing idea among the men. Can't blame the average middle-class man."

"But the expenses are at an all-time high anna."

"That's for you and Udit to figure out. Not me. Now if you'll excuse me, I have exactly 1400 vadas to make."

As Venkatesh rose to go to his kitchen, Jaseela noticed a glint in his eyes. So did Udit. He simply sat next to Jaseela and took her tea cup and drank the complete chocolate milk. He burped and then released an eight second long fart. Jaseela smiled to herself and took a bite of the biscuit in front of her. She then turned her head towards Udit with love teeming in her soul. But Udit was not there... Jaseela sat there, feeling more and more empty. How real that vision was... A voice could be heard now. It was calling out to her. It was a muffled sound. But a familiar one. Was that a dream too? No, it was not because Smitha was panting and shaking Jaseela on the shoulder trying to say, "Jaseela, you better come to the medical hut."

CHAPTER XXIV

Jasmine

Dr Jasmine Thomas had dreams about cinema. But her parents wanted her to be a nurse. They wanted her to do MBBS and fly to the UK or USA and get settled there. But what happened was that Jasmine ended up becoming a doctor practising general medicines. If her calling was the medical field, Jasmine wanted to become an oncologist. Fate placed her on this track. And she did make a lot of money. The rainy season was the best season. Not for sipping coffee in the cool rain sitting in the balcony making reels on the mobile phone. No. Jasmine would be barraged with parents of young school going children. Viral fever was Jasmine's hot enemy then. Of course, a host of other sicknesses did keep Jasmine on her toes.

She married a man named Thomas. So, for the progressives Jasmine hadn't changed her name post marriage. For the oldies, she was the modest wife who took on her husband's name. Thomas the husband was a pharmacist. He was a good man. It was Thomas who suggested Jasmine begin a clinic close to his pharmacy. It was a win-win situation. Between, Thomas had close friends in the film industry. And slowly Jasmine got to see some of her favourite film stars. Thomas, who would often get bit by the acting bug, got to show his face and talents on screen. Jasmine too felt she could give films a try.

But her stint with films would begin when Dr Putra the famous oncologist once presented himself at her clinic. He was having a severe headache. He was on his way with his family for a marriage. But the sudden attack of headache made him stop for some medicine to ease that head splitting pain. Getting to serve the legendary oncologist was never something Jasmine imagined. And she served him well. Jasmine even went one step further. She ran to Nair's café and told Nair to bring tea and his special samosa as fast as he could. When the tea arrived, Dr Putra was visibly surprised. "I came not to drink tea madam. Thank you for the medicine and the hospitality", said Dr Putra kindly. But Jasmine insisted he try the fuming tea. Fine, the old doctor tried the tea. He tried the tea almost 15 times. As he placed the empty cup on the table, he noticed his headache had gone.

Dr Putra was so impressed with Jasmine. He was sure there was something magical about Jasmine's way of treatment. And so, when Dr Putra was talking to one his patient's son, it was when Production Designer Kumar said The Rhino Emperor's second season was kickstarting soon and they needed an in-house doctor on set. Thomas was very excited. Jasmine was ok with the idea. She didn't want to be too close to those show off actors and film technicians. A distance was necessary. She had heard many great stories of humility and love about the film personalities. She had equally heard about grave and utterly heart-breaking stories as well. In the medical hut, Jasmine was shivering when she realised the fact that Srividya was actually pregnant. Jasmine didn't have the strength of heart to keep things like this vaulted within for the rest of her life. She wanted to run away.

Having sex was one's choice. But why pregnancy?? Jasmine's sister was on treatment to have children. The emotional distress was there to see. Her sister showered love upon Jasmine's children in such a way that the onlookers would think that the sister was the mother...

Here, some assholes fornicated. And the woman's womb had a life installed. God was so cruel. "Am I pregnant doctor?", enquired Srividya, weeping silently. Jasmine had somehow begun to like this cast and crew. No one behaved with a cinematic attitude to her. She had a special liking for Srividya who was always so full of life. But here she was on the bed, like a fallen decaying flower. Jasmine didn't know what to do. She went out of the tent as her eyes hunted for either Jaseela, Udit or Wendy. None were in sight.

CHAPTER XXV

Answers

Jaseela walked slowly, aimlessly. Yet she was panting. She had difficulty breathing. Smitha felt Jaseela's legs would flounder any moment. She had to lend support. Seeing a depressed Jaseela, Lucky Singh came to help as well. Jaseela craved Udit's presence. If she had never doubted him...

"What happened Jaseela? Looks like you saw a ghost or something", said Lucky with a genuine concern. By now several junior artists and crew members were seeing a weak Jaseela be almost carried by Lucky and followed by Smitha make their way to the medical hut. Jasmine, Anju, Roopa and Sharmeela were inside the hut. Sensing his presence was not needed, Lucky helped Jaseela to a seat and left. "Can I have some water?", enquired Jaseela feebly. Once she downed the water given by Anju in one large gulp, she wiped her face with her hands. Her hands ran through her dishevelled hair. She needed a bath. She was stinking from sweat. All the women in the hut were sweating. The whole set, the women and men and children all were sweating and smelling bad. Jaseela began to hate herself.

"Jaseela... Srividya is with child", said Jasmine making sure her voice didn't give out much emotion. She was shivering within. Srividya was still lying on the bed, weeping silently. All the other women now looked intently at Jaseela, the backbone of this entire show. Everyone felt she had an answer to the problem at hand. Jaseela was their leader. Jaseela was anything and everything each woman in that hut couldn't become. As for Jaseela, her mind had taken her trekking the Alps. Udit was with her. Two small children, resembling Udit and Jaseela, were tagging along. They lay down a blanket under an apple tree and had lunch. Jaseela made sure her children ate their fill. She smiled at her children, at her husband...

Jaseela's smile caught the women in the hut by surprise. Smitha shook Jaseela's shoulder once again. Jaseela regained her attention. All of a sudden, she got up and came close to Srividya and sitting on the bed, "Mohith?"

"Heyson...", came the answer.

"Jaseela... What if the media comes to know?", asked Smitha with fear in her voice.

"I don't know Smitha. I don't know..."

"That asshole must marry her", said Anju in an angry tone.

Except for Jaseela, everyone in the hut knew that the sex between Srividya and Heyson was not out of love. But no one knew that Supriya and Heyson had forced Srividya into the sex. Srividya didn't want to mention that angle. She was afraid. Jasmine wanted to quit her job. She felt so repulsed. She wanted to vomit. She wanted to run to her husband and cry onto his shoulders. Sharmeela saw the demons surface again. Anju clenched her fists in helplessness. Smitha felt her own stomach and reminisced about the moment when she came to know she was pregnant for the first time. How thrilled her husband and she were. Jaseela felt numb. Just then Kannaki entered the hut. All the women in the hut hated Kannaki. She was ok with that. Kannaki herself despised her life.

"Heyson came to my room and confessed. The gutless bastard was hiding in the toilet... He is presently crying in my room... Look, I have seen these kinds of scenes several times before... I made Supriya to force Srividya into doing it with Heyson... I made her to do it... But I didn't know it would turn this ugly."

Dead silence. No one heard the last line delivered by Kannaki. Rather, everyone could hear the silent breathing of everyone else. Then, Anju started walking towards Kannaki, each step made with rage. Anju's eyes were flushing with anger and tears when she stood in front of Kannaki. She wanted to slap Kannaki. She wanted to stab Kannaki in the heart, at that spot. Anju began crying and fell to the floor. She beat the floor angrily. Sharmeela and Smitha sat down near Anju. All this time there was Roopa standing in a corner, not able to comprehend the levels of intimacy that crisscrossed the frugal lives of these human beings.

"To Srividya... Heyson is already engaged. To some MLA's daughter. You have no chance to be with him. I don't think any sane man will accept you in this condition. The good-natured woman that you are, I don't think you will want another man to become that child's father...", said Kannaki and she held her tongue for a few seconds. As everyone now looked at Kannaki intently, she continued, "By now you must have got the gist of what I am trying to convey... That is the only option in front of you Srividya", said Kannaki. Her voice was shivering when she spoke the last part with tears welling up in her eyes. Anju replied in an angry tone, "How easy for a pimp to say that. You vile woman..."

With a sudden smile, the teary-eyed Kannaki said, "It is easy for me... because I was in Srividya's place... When I was just 16 years old... I was all alone with some man's child inside my stomach... Seeing all of you supporting Srividya I feel jealous. I had no one to speak to, to cry with... My first child... I still have dreams of that unborn child. But... never in those dreams have I seen my baby's face..."

Kannaki wiped away her tears. Eating down that intense internal pain she looked at the weakened Jaseela and switching to her old defiant self instantly, Kannaki said, "If all the women simply sit here, the junior artists and all outside will begin to feel something is off. We don't want that. This is not the information the world wants to know about The Rhino Emperor. I will start the damage control process. Srividya has loose motion. She ate something bad. Her stomach went berserk. This is the story... We need to feed the extras and then get them out of this set by 2 PM. Now girls, get on with it!"

Clapping her hands loudly, Kannaki left the medical hut. Silence ensued. Silence amid that mental chaos. Along with that silence, a deep and profound sense of respect began growing in the hearts of the women present there, towards Kannaki. The hatred they had harboured in their minds against that one woman simply vanished, just like that. They hadn't experienced anything close to what Kannaki had said... Jaseela and then later on, the others including Srividya, slowly walked out of the hut. They had work to do. Jasmine sat on her chair and wiped the tears from her cheek.

CHAPTER XXVI

Meet

The press meet began with why Bhagath lit fire to almost 20% of the set. Why did he go berserk? Was he intoxicated? Why was there a spat between Jaseela and Bhagath prior to the trial shoot? Was it true that Bhagath was rude with his co-actors and crew? Was it true that some actors in the series signed for the second season without knowing anything about the intimate scenes and body exhibitions to be made? Why were they not informed about such scenes beforehand? What was the intimacy coordinator doing when an actor apparently touched the stomach of a female actor without her consent during the trial shoot?

Jaseela was aware that the journalists would try to throw her off course just like that. The last query was one such. Nothing like that had happened on the set... Or was she unaware of such incidents? How could she be so oblivious to such happenings? After all, that single shot was just part of a make-belief. She could have thought about that ending scene in a traditional manner. She was adamant, full to the brim with ego. Jaseela wanted a place in history, a legacy. That was all she cared about. Jaseela knew she was the heartless tyrant king Jeyopola... Yet, only then did she notice; both her and his names began with the letter J and ended with the letter A.

"Why were you not willing to answer the calls that came across to you for around two weeks?", asked one journalist.

With an uninterested attitude Jaseela replied saying, "I needed confirmations. I cannot speak to the media just with half-baked stories. Moreover, the studio executives took off. I didn't see that coming. They too had the responsibility to be here."

"Now the junior artist's pregnancy has been confirmed says reports. Have you any comment on that?"

"I don't understand how that becomes my problem?"

"The offer to a better future was given in your set. The cameraman, Mr Heyson Prasanna, was working for you. Is it not strange that the junior artists, especially the female junior artists, do not have any security over their bodies in a series helmed by a woman?"

"I am given the responsibility to write and direct one of the biggest series our nation has ever seen. Do you think I will have the time to think about anything else? And from what I gather, there was no physical struggle between the accused and the victim. Which to me means it was consensual. Which again tells about how they were ok with that physical union. How am I going to stop that?"

"Does your agreement stipulate anything about physical unions?"

"Yes, there are clauses that state that sexual activities must not be done within the sets. Forceful sex, if proven to be right, will lead to severe legal actions. The victim has already said it was consensual."

"Is it true that the cameraman used to misbehave with the female actors and crew?"

"I can sincerely say that none of such issues have come to my attention. Being a woman, I myself have not had any bad experiences from the accused."

"Just because you had no such experiences doesn't rule out the chance that the accused didn't misbehave with his female colleagues."

"I... See, My mind had been filled with that single shot's..."

"Sorry for interrupting ma'am, but there is invalidated information that alleges the CEO of Little Further Up having accosted you in an indecent manner, not once but several times. Do you wish to comment on that?"

Jaseela knew she had to face the questions the media people threw at her, alone. There was so much pride running in her blood. None of the executives from Little Further Up were ready to meet the media. Jonathan didn't return from London. Tim and Wendy quit. Despite the constant requests and support from her trustable crew and cast, Jaseela decided to handle the media on her own. Even as everyone else accepted Jaseela's decision, Udit still went. He sat with Jaseela through those gruelling minutes. He had not been with her during the trial shoot, one of the biggest moments in Jaseela's life. How supremely idiotic he had been to work out an ego clash at that critical moment. He knew Jaseela. They could have talked it out. Instead, Udit simply walked away. Not this time. He had agreed to remain silent. That was Jaseela's order. Still, within, Jaseela was happy Udit was there with her now.

It was true that Jaseela never knew about the sexual escapades exhibited by some of the members of the series. She was not aware of Heyson's misbehaviour with some female crew members. She was in some sort of trance, a comfortable bubble that she conjured to shield her creativity and maybe even her existence itself. Jaseela was so engrossed with the thought of that single shot, she was inadvertently becoming Jeyopola; just wanting to win no matter what. Jaseela chastised herself. She had failed as a director, as a team captain, as a lover, as a friend, as a woman... Amidst her ruminations and replies to the media, the breaking news broke the backbone of The Rhino Emperor, sealing its fate.

CHAPTER XXVII

Tenth

Kannaki took Srividya away from the set secretly at sun down. She had made calls to a local hospital in the Andhra-Kolaazham border. The doctor knew Kannaki. For Rs 5 lakhs the job would be done. Srividya said nothing. She complied. She went without any feelings visible on her face. Within, she was probably burning. Heyson came out of the toilet about four hours after the trial shoot ended. He didn't know what the scene was outside. Apparently, no one seemed to be indifferent to him. That was a welcome relief. He began looking for Srividya. Heyson wanted to talk to her. He didn't see her after the trial shot. Maybe she was waiting for him somewhere. He decided to keep looking. His steps were faltering. He had heard the rest of the day had been called off. He went to Kannaki.

Walking through the set, Jaseela felt she was on the brink of derangement. One more negative news and she knew her sane mind was history. What weakened this woman of steel? Certainly, Udit's departure was not the reason. Jaseela simply couldn't acknowledge that. She had faced tough times even before Udit came into her life. Jaseela didn't want to lay down her existence at anyone's feet for her to survive on this planet. Yes she needed love, companionship, support... She was a human being. She was not an independent woman. But she wasn't dependent on anyone per se. No one needed to depend on her either. She voiced her concerns, her doubts... Udit left because he was an escapist Jaseela felt.

Venkatesh sat in the village square set as he now noticed the film set of The Rhino Emperor. It was utter chaos. No one knew what to do. There was no one to head the problems at hand. Venkatesh thought about the 1400 vadas he had made. He was really looking forward to Bhagath's reaction and comment on those vadas when Venkatesh actually gave him them. Now that occasion had gone, never to return probably. Venkatesh's loneliness was disturbed by Jaseela who came and sat next to him.

"Kannaki has connections. She will do the needful. She'll take Srividya in the evening", said Jaseela as she sat down near Venkatesh. "Did you make the 1400 vadas anna?"

"Unlike that Kannaki the fraud who will take advantage of men... I actually made the 1400 vadas. I don't feign."

"Hmm... At this moment, I don't know what would have happened had Kannaki not been here with us on this set. She is a woman with a strong heart anna. I thought I was strong. I am not. There is so much to learn from Kannaki..."

Silence.

"So... Will this set be dismantled soon?"

"Nothing of that sort has been decided anna. We haven't heard from the financing company. I had known about Wendy's wish to handle the direction and writing of this series. She can take it if she wants to, if the company thinks I am not efficient enough."

"And then what will you do my child?"

"What is your plan anna? I'll come with you. I am tired of film making."

"Cooking is even more tiring my dear."

"Then what should I do anna?"

"For a start, go hug that stupid fellow coming to us."

Jaseela raised her eyes to the direction where Venkatesh had turned his head. It was towards the iron gate of the walled city. The afternoon sun was hot. Through the smoke, dust and commotion a figure was walking slowly with a perfect pace. Jaseela knew who that figure was. Yet she sat there imagining the end of season two as she had it in her mind: a defeated Jeyopola with the wobbly stomach entering the city amid smoke, dust and commotion. No one noticed the tyrant king as it was written so in the screenplay. No one noticed Udit even as he neared Jaseela. How the two lovers would react to each other scared Venkatesh who got up and walked away. Udit patted Jaseela's head softly and sat next to her. She moved closer to Udit. They sat there watching the chaotic extras on the set being led out of the set after lunch.

Birbal and Sharmeela sat in the royal hall all quiet. The commotion outside was maddening. Birbal looked at the spot where he had to kneel as Walika. Sharmeela looked at the spot where she had to lay down as Jeyopola defiled her character. They had performed their characters with much energy during the trial shoot just a few hours ago... A few hours ago. Who would have thought things would take an unprecedented turn as this. Sharmeela told Birbal Kannaki had arranged Srividya to be taken to a hospital in the Andhra border where *it* would be done. The images of their children crossed Birbal's mind. Sharmeela and Birbal sat there brooding. Then Sharmeela told her husband about the things Kannaki told. There was a sense of loss evident on Bribal's face.

Kannaki had the uphill task of making the entire cast and crew understand and cooperate lest the production of a great television series be mocked at. She knew history would look at Heyson in the most detestable manner. He would be hated. It was anyway of his own doing. Kannaki set him up with Srividya. The idea of impregnating her was his own choice. Heyson had to pay for that crime... And Srividya had a bright future in films. She had to stay strong. Kannaki was praying to all the gods now, after neglecting them for about 18 years. She wanted Srividya to bounce back. Kannaki had made all her plans. The naïve person that Srividya was, she would require a heartless manager. Kannaki was that manager. Kannaki adored Srividya's sensuous body. Kannaki could land Srividya several projects. She would heed... All that would happen only if Srividya came through strongly. Kannaki sat in the car, ruminating and occasionally turning back to see how Srividya was faring.

The 500 extras left by 2:15 PM. Most of the crew were also instructed to take a week's off. And then there was silence. Sitting in the canteen, Kumar was sipping a black tea as he daydreamed in that relentlessly hot afternoon. His dream was in slow-motion: the 8 Kg prosthetic wobbly stomach lay on the ground. A teenage boy and few of his friends who were part of the defeated city's citizen characters, were carefully confiscating artefacts from the set. The boy took the stomach. But being the wobbly item it was, he dropped it and went another way. Kumar had no interest in safe keeping his beloved set and the innumerable artefacts his team and he had made. All this was ending, had ended. Now who bothered as to what happened. He took the wobbly stomach and started walking to Smitha's department... He was among the few crew members who actually knew nothing about the issues that had really occurred. He didn't in fact. He wanted to work with Jaseela. And that's all that mattered. And so, his answers to the questions posed were actually genuine. He was happy to see Jaseela and Udit had come back together. It was a pain to see them go separate ways.

Costume designer Fathima and Stunt master Lucky came and sat near Kumar. Venkatesh came with two glasses of black tea. He too sat with them with a glass of black tea. There were vadas on the table. The four drank their tea and ate the vadas. Then Kumar said in a feeble voice,

"You know, my wife lost her life to lung cancer. Funny right? I used to smoke, a lot. And here I am. I often think I made Ragini breathe in all that toxic smoke from the cigarettes... My daughter was only 13 when Ragini went. Now my child is 25. Twelve years ago Ragini... You know when she left, I was overcome with grief so deep, I would even forget about my daughter. For days she would be with Jaseela's parents. They loved my child. They took care of her. I would never go to work, just sleeping the days through. I lost my job as the art and crafts teacher of... haha I forgot the school's name... And then you know, almost a month later, Jaseela calls me and says she is planning her debut film and she wants me in it as the production designer... Jaseela saved me... But something within tells me I cannot save her from this fiasco."

"Probably the casting agency will file a complaint with the local police station. If that happens, then all of us will be questioned", spoke Lucky who then continued saying, "After Jonathan reinstated Kannaki and her accomplices, I knew there would be a downward spiral."

Fathima voiced her concern saying, "I hope this series continues its journey. I mean this is our livelihood now right? If all this just stops one day, how will we feed our kids? I have a treatment to take that itself costs a lot. A few loans."

"Probably Jaseela will get a suspension", contemplated Kumar.

"Watch out for that Wendy", said Venkatesh.

"If Wendy takes on this series, I'll leave. Period", pitched in Fathima in a gross manner.

Fathima's words and expressions were very comical that the four people simply laughed out loud. They needed a relief. But within, the men too had Fathima's opinion. They too would leave the project if Wendy came on board as writer/director. But they also knew that that would be suicide as quitting would amount to huge financial distress for the entire team associated with The Rhino Emperor. Finishing his vada Lucky said, "My children were so thrilled when I told them about Jaseela's offer to me in this series. Frankly I didn't know much about Jaseela's early works. I was going to say no to the offer when one day the kids simply decided to not go to school you know why? They wanted to show me some of Jaseela's films. We watched I think three of her films from morning to evening. And boy was that a revelation. That woman is literally cinema incarnate I tell you... My children are the reason I am here right now. I feel proud I listened to my children's words. Or else I would have missed out a lifetime's opportunity. It'll be sad if Jaseela gets replaced."

The time moved to 6 PM. Kannaki had left with Srividya. The lights on the set were switched on by Kumar who then came and sat near the lovers in the village square. Just then Devaprasad Rai arrived at the set. He came up to the trio and somehow seated himself close to them. No one spoke. They only had Jeyopola in mind. They knew for certain Jeyopola now would remain only in their minds. Tim and Wendy came to the spot. "Heard you are getting married", said Kumar to them.

"Yes, we are Kumar", replied Wendy. "We have our futures to look to, right?"

"This was our future Wendy. And now it's gone probably", said Kumar pointing out to the whole set.

Wendy felt relieved seeing Udit was back. The cast and crew were confused; should they remain on set or leave? Srividya went to her aunty's home was the information spread out. By then Smitha, Lucky Singh, Fathima and Jasmine and most of the crew came to the village square. Heyson walked up to the group. No one talked to him. Everyone was silent. As Tim and Wendy arrived at the spot, no one had noticed that they were absent from the trial shoot. Tim broke the silence.

"Guys... We have an announcement to make..."

Everyone looked up at the couple. Tim continued,

"We are getting married. Wendy is carrying my child."

With disgust Jaseela quipped, "You sure that's yours Tim?"

"Jaseela don't make this ugly. You are lucky you aren't carrying *his* child", quipped Wendy.

"And I didn't... Neither did I backstab anyone for your kind information."

"You are not the only ambitious woman in this world Jaseela... And you have had your share of men. You have Udit now... I need a life. I too have ambitions. Not all of us are built to be like you Jaseela...", said Wendy with a sad shivering voice.

"Let us not belittle ourselves now. I have known both Wendy and Jaseela from the institute days. You women are feisty, are ambitious, are lovable... If you can't see common ground now, fine. Go your separate ways. But I do wish you can remain friends", said Udit sincerely.

Before anyone could speak further, they all heard a scream. It was Bhagath. He was heavily drunk. He was holding a piece of log that was on fire. One of the shops up front, near the gate was on fire. Bhagath now began to run. He was mad with anger. Everyone at the square was confused; were they seeing Jeyopola or Bhagath? In that confusion they didn't notice Bhagath run up to Heyson and ram him to the ground. Heyson fell with a thud. Lucky Singh tried to pull Bhagath away. But he felt so surprised with the strength the man had. Bhagath pushed away Lucky and began beating Heyson on the face and chest. He was mad with anger. Almost all present knew what the retaliation was about. Heyson too. He didn't react. The fire in the set began to spread. Udit contacted the fire department immediately. Tim contacted the police.

Bhagath was taken into custody for attempted murder and destruction of property. Heyson was rushed to the hospital. Luckily there weren't any serious life-threatening injuries. Heyson needed two weeks' rest. Bhagath was remanded. The preproduction work of The Rhino Emperor's second season stalled. The entire production came to a grinding halt when Kannaki called up Heyson one day around two weeks later. She said the job had been done. There was deep contempt in her voice. She thought he would accept the pregnancy. Rather he went and hid in the toilet. Kannaki yelled at him for never visiting Srividya even once, in those crucial hours. If he had, Srividya would probably be a happy woman now. Now, she was like a statue. Somehow the half-born mother in Srividya was trying to survive despite the reality of no child to care for. But fate made matters worse, in the form of Heyson's indifference that day. Kannaki regretted having forged a friendship with Heyson.

Heyson accepted whatever Kannaki said, with patience. He regretted his actions. He knew he would be haunted by that unborn child for the rest of his life. The tears flowing from his eyes were burning his cheeks. Heyson cut Kannaki's call before she could continue yelling out her pain. Heyson stepped onto the balcony. For a second the thought that he was residing on the tenth floor of the apartment building amused him...

The tenth floor... The tenth elephant...

CHAPTER XXVIII

Fire

The shock on Jonathan's face was palpable. From the other end of the phone, Tim had delivered the news. He wanted to tell Jonathan that he and Wendy were going to tie the knot and that they were going to quit from The Rhino Emperor. But he didn't want to be branded a backstabber. Moreover, Heyson's suicide was a much bigger news to be told. The major people in the cast and crew had already come to know about Heyson's hasty decision to end his life. Bhagath, who loved Srividya like his own daughter, had bashed Heyson several times in his mind even more. Bhagath had lost control of himself. He was drunk. He would have ruptured Heyson's rib cage had Lucky Singh not intervened.

Bhagath was taken into police custody for attempted murder and destruction of property. With a bloodied face and body Heyson was being carried to an ambulance. All he could see now was Srividya being carried on the tenth elephant. Heyson's mind was urging him to rise and run into the kitchen and lock himself in the room where kerosene was usually kept. Within, in his mind, Heyson had immolated himself.

Jonathan cut the phone call. He sat in his office, trying hard to breathe. His eyes were bulging out. His nerves were cracking. His head was beginning to swirl. He didn't expect this news; this surprise. His mind couldn't handle that horrific surprise. Throughout the next week, Jonathan began seeing visions. There was death everywhere he looked. There was Heyson's young face wherever he looked. Oh, how much Jonathan had tormented Heyson. Heyson's allegiance to Jonathan spelled his last. Jonathan knew he was the reason for Heyson's death. On the seventh day after Heyson's death, and despite the winter cool in the atmosphere of London, Jonathan was sweating profusely, the day his mind slipped into total insanity. His jealousy towards Jaseela, nay, his want for 'justice' was the starting point of all this. Was he The Rhino Emperor? Was he the heartless Jeyopola? Time had given him the answer... The news that went out was Heyson had impregnated a junior artist. He had violated her. That deep remorse was what led him to take his life and that Bhagath intervened when he came to know of the situation. Kannaki arranged a junior artist to take on the responsibility of the pregnancy for an amount of Rs 25 lakhs. The junior artist who was facing sexual harassment for over a year from several people in several film sets, pounced onto this deal but venting out her anger through that huge amount. She had to stay away from the public for two years. The junior artist accepted the condition happily.

Jonathan had his team sanction the amount in secret through Tim. Jonathan wanted to call Jaseela or Wendy or Udit... He knew no one would take his call. Eventually he dialled his wife Elsa frantically who had just returned home from an invigorating sex session with a classmate from school whom she met at the shopping centre. Elsa was dumbstruck hearing her estranged husband cry feverishly. Elsa tried to calm him. She took a cab and made it to Jonathan's office. As she ran into Jonathan's office room, he was holding the glass window's handle in his hand, his head tilted to the road ten storeys down. Elsa made slow steps towards her husband holding her breath. She was scared. She didn't want her children's father to commit suicide.

Some part of her did really love him. That part in her now touched Jonathan. He fell to the floor and wept. Elsa sat down next to him and took his weeping head and placed it on her lap. She caressed his hair and waited with tears welled in her eyes for Jonathan to open up. A cold wind began to blow gently into the room.

A shivering Jonathan collected as much strength as he could garner and spoke to Elsa about all the happenings, from the beginning, that finally culminated in the cancelling of The Rhino Emperor and the suicide of a young man. There was blood on his hands, claimed Jonathan. He kept repeating the term 'blood on my hands', swinging his head back and forth. Flashes of Walika's hanging children's corpses came to his mind. Those corpses were swinging back and forth in the gentle breeze Jaseela said, during the narration. One of those children was Heyson. The other was Srividya. The third was Jaseela. They were all going to die starting with Heyson. Jonathan got up all of a sudden and screamed 'blood on my hands' and ran out. He ran hysterically. There was no stopping him. All the employees stood with hairs on their arms all risen and with gaping mouths as they saw their boss descend into total madness. Elsa did not budge from her position. She knew for a fact that she had lost her husband completely as the panic-stricken voice of Jonathan could be heard in the background screaming out 'Jeyopola Udit Jaseela Wendy Walika Tim Heyson Kannaki Srividya Bhagath The Rhino Emperor!!'.

CHAPTER XXIX

Death

"Do celebrities clean their own toilets?", asked a student amid the crowd's laughter. Jaseela could feel the irritability in that stupid question. Still, with a smile she answered, "That I am not sure about. But when I was part of a television series production, I would still clean my toilet... Even today, oh ya today was my husband's turn to clean the toilet. I was in charge of cooking... So, I guess... Um, please do ask questions based on the topic assigned please. Thank you."

"What is cinema to you ma'am?", enquired an energetic college student. Jaseela saw her younger self somewhere lurking within that girl. Jaseela smiled. She thought for a second. That second but lasted an eternity. In that one second Jaseela's mind took her on a journey that, like a slideshow, projected Jaseela's life till that point. All those happenings. The cooking stints with her father at the film sets, the women centric films, The Rhino Emperor, Udit, Bhagath, Kannaki, the infamous long duration single shot... Jonathan...

"Cinema to me... It is the moment you step into the set of the film that was existing in your mind up till then. That is cinema. You see, cinema is a conglomeration of various factors. Take your college for example. Take this film studies class for example. We all had to come together; someone had to know someone else blah blah blah... Here we are. I'm sure the organisers of this film-based seminar series will be glad to know how successful the project has turned out. Yes, I can see the happy faces of the teachers and students behind this endeavour... the idea to bring seven major film personalities and then me as well haha to your midst is a daunting task. You know these film people. They don't have a fixed date for anything. Things keep changing. Again, that is life... Cinema is a reflection of that change, that constant flux. So, as I said earlier, cinema is what you conceived in the mind and how you bring it to life. It all begins with the story and then how you want to present the story. Then comes who you would want to portray the characters, the cast... who would aptly portray what you have written down. You also need the crew who can feel what you felt when you stood in those imaginary streets, on that battlefield, that old tree house into which the morning sunshine entered through the creaks and cracks and where one character proposed to their sweetheart... You see, all these situations require different kinds of lighting and costumes. The tricky part would be with the camera department. You have a handful of well-defined shots and you need to carefully use those shots which will definitely repeat themselves throughout the entire length of the film the audience is watching. And still the camera angles shouldn't feel repetitive. That is a gargantuan task... But do you know where cinema is actually born? Exactly, at the editing desk. Good one dear. You'll make a good editor one day... Yes, I said earlier that standing on the set of your film that you had in your mind for a long time was cinema... But here, when you begin to see all the elements finally being stitched together... When the film is beginning to come to life you know shot by shot, scene by scene... The film is coming to life. It's your baby right. The baby is coming to life. Stretching its legs, wondering what had happened and what is now. The moment the baby lets out its first cry is the same as when we watch our film, the first cut. No embellishments. And yet, there it is... Your baby... amidst all the blood and whatnots... I always like to think that The Rhino Emperor is my first child. I have been blessed with three children. The younger two are probably home now after their school, being pampered by their father haha... My first child? It's still beating within. It's still there in my womb... All this, dear students are the romanticising part of films. If you really want to be a film maker you should know how to deal with people. That one major factor is of prime importance. And that you'll know once you enter the industry... Thank you."

Jaseela decided to take the Kolaazham Metro to reach her home. Despite the insistence that the students drop her, Jaseela wanted to see her homeland so eagerly. What had changed? Literally nothing. This was a relief to Jaseela. Of late she was afraid of change. Jaseela would get up in the morning and view the tiny hands and legs of her two children. She didn't want her children to grow up. She lost her innocent first child. She didn't want to lose her other two children to this cruel world... Ludicrous thoughts... Jaseela was a selfish parent... Regarding the last words she spoke in the seminar; The Rhino Emperor was still in her womb? Why was she so dramatic? Yes, she loved her series, her creation. But was that creation actually her first child? Or was she just making it up to get good reviews from the students who would feel sorry for her despite the expert talk she gave, which would then lead to more seminars in other schools and colleges... Jaseela needed the money desperately.

After the second season got stalled due to the pregnancy debacle, Heyson's suicide and Jonathan's fall into insanity, the executives fired Jaseela and the entire crew. They were willing to go ahead with Wendy as the writer/director and the existing cast. But no one was willing to work with Wendy and Tim. Moreover, Bhagath was sentenced to ten years' imprisonment. He told the court he had planned to murder Heyson that day; he was angry. Bhagath's confession sent shockwaves in the television and cinema industry. The Rhino Emperor thus got the red signal. Production stopped. All the agreements lapsed. And the major blow came when Elsa, Jonathan's wife who took over the reins of Little Further Up decided not to honour the remunerations due to the cast and crew.

No one, except Tim and Wendy, ever got a single Rupee as remuneration from that mammoth project's second season. Tim and Wendy were doing well in the UK. Wendy had her own sitcom going too well. The Beef Steaks, Wendy's creation, was contesting the Emmys this year. Smitha went back into the cake business. Kumar started a wedding decoration firm. Lucky Singh Rajput had a gym already. And he was the personal trainer of several television actors. Jasmine still had her clinic running. Roopa got married and settled in New Delhi. She left the field and started taking tuitions. Birbal took up every acting deal. He took whatever came his way, even B films. Sharmeela stopped acting and she now assisted Smitha in the cake business. That was sweeter and rewarding. Though she got other acting offers, Anju decided to concentrate all her energy into developing her school for the under-privileged children in her area. The classes were often handled by her cast and crew friends. Fathima opened a boutique. Her 'Viking' saree was an instant hit. She kept churning out remarkable designs and custom-made wear for the ladies. Kannaki was the manager of the star Srividya who had just won her second National Award. Srividya was on a winning streak. Just five years after the shutting down of The Rhino Emperor, the cute and naive Srividya had transformed miraculously into the reigning female lead in South India. She was going to foray into Bollywood soon. There were rumours that she was dating Mohith... Where was Mohith Jaseela thought, on that day of the trial shoot? She clearly remembered he was there in position near the first elephant, on his assigned horse. Where did he go after the trial?

Devaprasad Rai, Venkatesh, Lavanya and Jaseela's mother had passed on in a gap of three years after the series got scrapped. Sitting in the Koletro, Jaseela smiled to herself as she recollected her talks and debates with Venkatesh. He came relatively at the fag end of The Rhino Emperor's existence. But he made such a mark on the people around him, that Jaseela often visualised Venkatesh in mind whenever she got confused or depressed with life. Venkatesh had a knack to life. His formula was to look at life like the boiling oil in a kadai. Like the oil which would eventually turn dark after being immersed with various foods to be cooked and fried, our lives too would darken as we immersed ourselves in the experiences that life threw onto us. But unlike the darkening oil, if we had the right mindset, our minds wouldn't darken. Rather, it would brighten. As an example, Venkatesh would smile. He had no teeth in the front. That was comical. But his confidence was what mattered. Venkatesh never shied away from laughing out loud. That was the brightening moment.

Lavanya had finally made peace with her son when she met him for the last time, in jail. Lavanya had issues walking. Her old legs couldn't carry her body weight. Yet, Lavanya made it a point to see her son every month. And Bhagath soon became eager to see his mother every month.

Bhagath was immensely surprised how his feelings for his parents had changed; his parents simply loved him. It was toxic. But, with Lavanya almost ready to move on, Bhagath wanted to spend as much time as he could, with his mother. It was not that he regretted what he did. He was a stoic. And when he finally lit the funeral pyre, Bhagath did not cry. He had found peace at last. He still had his wife and three daughters now, and his sister as well. The superstar Srividya was one of the only three people who Bhagath wanted to see while in jail. And Srividya would often visit Bhagath. He was among the very few people whom she respected. He went to jail for her. The orphan never thought anyone could be that selfless.

Jaseela's mother had the luck of having seen her new two grandchildren before breathing her last. When Udit and Jaseela signed in the book in the register office, Jaan was the happiest mother in the world. She didn't know much about feminism. She was old school. But she knew a person with a heart and soul needed a companion. She knew Jaseela was a strong person. But her heart and mind were not always strong. Udit was her support. Jaan loved Udit.

Devaprasad Rai composed music for two more projects before laying down his favourite harmonium that served him for forty-five years. The projects were films. He lobbied for Jaseela, not because she requested him to do so, but of his own accord. But by then, the superstitious film industry had already branded Jaseela a bad luck, post The Rhino Emperor debacle. Rai had great concern for Jaseela and her friends, all who got greatly affected by the debacle. Even as Devaprasad Rai's health started decaying faster as he neared his death, Rai proposed a project, a love story between a prostitute and a musician, wherein

Jaseela wrote and directed it and her crew and cast from the series could be part of the film. He wanted to produce the film. That dream project was taken up by Jaseela excitedly. Devaprasad Rai began composing for his swansong project when he passed away. His head was resting peacefully on the keys of his beloved harmonium. Jaseela felt half her heart, her very own existence, had been torn away from her ruthlessly when she came to know of Rai's demise. She didn't attend his funeral.

CHAPTER XXX

Rage

The financial blockade imposed by Elsa turned to severe financial problems for all the people involved. Several education loans, housing loans, vehicle loans, insurance policy renewals, school fees, daily grocery buying etc all went for a toss. Jaseela's Rs 8 Cr salary from The Rhino Emperor just vanished into thin air when Elsa decided to go for the extreme act. She had known all along about the sexual relation between Jaseela and Jonathan. And when fate was in her hands, Elsa reacted without any human concern. She single-handedly destroyed the lives of several people. Little Further Up closed their offices in India.

Jaseela took all the small opportunities that came her way. The latest seminar about films had given her a chance to go to some colleges in Kerala next month, to deliver talks on cinema. Life was good but life was tougher than she had fathomed. Udit was trying his best to make ends meet as well. But there wasn't much money to pay for house maids. And the growing age of the children meant someone had to stay home. Udit volunteered. Jaseela agreed. He took tuitions, helped school children with their short film projects, dreamt in secret about his pet project, took care of the children superbly, cooked and cleaned the flat.

Jaseela was sweating by the time she reached her apartment's steps. No one was around. She passed wind, took out her purse and opened the envelope that was given by the college authorities after the seminar. A cheque of Rs 30,000. Not bad. But she expected more. Jaseela had come to expect more of late. She was dejected. She entered her flat. Just then a party popper burst into the air. Jaseela let out a shriek. As she came to her senses, she saw Smitha, Fathima, Kumar, Lucky, Jasmine, Mitra, Sharmeela, Birbal and Udit scream 'Happy Birthday Jaseela'. All the kids were running around. The planning had begun a week back. Everyone would make some food item and bring it to Jaseela's home. Through a conference video call, Roopa and Kannaki had joined. Jasmine had joined the gang. Though she wanted to forget the series, she wanted this union of friends.

That night all the bleakness that surrounded the lives of those humans had gone away. It felt like they were on a film set. They even came up with a dummy film story and each department explained their ideas. Jaseela gave her ideas. Producer Udit dropped the project. A huge laughter erupted in the group. It was decided then that every month this reunion would be conducted. Udit and Jaseela wanted that reunion to be held in their flat as it was easily accessible. The group went into complaining mode as they aimed and fired missiles at Elsa, Tim and Wendy. They thought about Heyson and Bhagath. The birthday session ended at 9 PM. The friends left. After the children were put to sleep, Jaseela took the initiative to have an intimate session with Udit who readily agreed. That night, in the living room, under hushed sounds the wife and husband had a roller coaster ride. Udit took out all that he had from his arsenal. Jaseela didn't give up easily... As the couple lay in each other's arms panting and stinking from the sweat, Udit said, "Jaseela, remember my Tamil screenplay Kaala Kaapathungo?"

"Ya that slapstick comedy, right?"

"Yes. Seems Andromeda Films is interested in the project. A deal may be signed next week."

Jaseela stopped breathing as she raised her head towards Udit. Her eyes were bulging in utter surprise. She began to hope again. She kissed him tightly. Then,

"Are you sure about the deal Udit?"

"Yes my love. It is going to happen."

"My birthday is your lucky day then Udit... Shouldn't we celebrate this news?"

Udit nodded his head in approval and a second session of intense love making ensued. All that time his mind was filled with the sensuousness of Jaseela's body. But in parallel there was that constant feel of disgust seeping into his gut, into his soul. It was Kumar who had suggested Andromeda Films to Udit. Kumar had come to know that that group was planning to produce a film if the screenplay was worth the money. Language was not an issue. Though, they did prefer a South Indian language. Udit called Andromeda's office. Kumar had made prior calls. The meeting was arranged without any hassles. Udit had asked Kumar to keep a lid on this topic until something credible and concrete happened. That was why Kumar didn't mention anything about that topic during Jaseela's birthday party.

Udit was ushered into the room. The room was modest. Within, the AC's cooling was incredible. Udit was reminded of the coolness Jeyopola felt when he entered the royal hall of Chaapikia. Udit sat on the chair assigned and he waited. He was holding his breath. There was tension slowly simmering in him. He had doubts about this idea, about the screenplay. After that harrowing experience at the Equator Hotel, he never visited the screenplay. That was about eight years ago. What an idiot Udit was to not go through his writings. There would be enough material to be cut out and new ideas to be incorporated.

Instead, Udit just brushed off the dust that had laid to rest on the top skin of the file which contained his screenplay. The opening of the door hastened the beating of Udit's heart. A lady, in her 50s, came in and sat on her chair. She was Andrea Almeda, the owner of Andromeda Films. She was a good-looking woman. Udit saw a confident woman sitting in front of him; the same attitude he craved to see in Jaseela these days. Andrea and Udit exchanged a few pleasantries. Then,

"It was heart breaking to know that The Rhino Emperor was getting scrapped. I loved the violence and sex shown in the show. Your wife had a great vision and guts to depict such scenes. Bhagath was a great choice for the central character. He was or still is a good friend though I haven't seen him since he went to jail... All right, shall we get down to business?"

And Udit, after taking a deep breath, started to narrate his story. Udit felt really confident as Andrea listened intently to each and every word he said. She laughed heartily listening to the comedy scenes. She was actually on the edge of the seat when scenes of intrigue and suspense were talked about. Nearing the climax, she got up with suspense filling the air. Andrea could sit no more. Finally, catharsis... Andrea gave out a clap. Wow! This lady really loved Udit's screenplay and his narration especially. Yes, things were going to get better. All the financial troubles were going to be something of the past. Udit had reached the point where he cared nothing about his passion for cinema. All he wanted was a better life for Jaseela and the children. Udit too rose from his seat.

"I am quite impressed with you Udit. Maybe one more round of narration you know with my husband will be necessary. He couldn't make it today. Can you come tomorrow?"

Udit narrated his screenplay with the same zeal and zest to Andrea's husband the very next day. The husband was even more expressive than Andrea. Fate had finally shown Udit a way out. One door had finally opened. And Andrea closed it and locked the door. Udit knew he got locked as well. Upon meeting Udit over a few meetings, Andrea had begun to have feelings for him. She knew he wouldn't reciprocate her feelings. And she also knew how desperate Udit was to get this project on the road. She knew he would comply. She didn't like rough men. Udit was her kind of man; the submissive type.

And so, when Andrea locked the door the first time, Udit complied. The same man who put off a physical union with the woman of his life until marriage, was selling his body to another woman so that he could provide a better life for his family. But he knew he had to show genuine interest in Andrea or else all that he dreamt of would simply wash down the drain. Thus, Udit went along with Andrea. He made sure she got what she wanted. Andrea for her part, was good enough to take the project one step at a time forward for each session with Udit. Andrea knew Udit was burning inside and she loved it. She loved it when men got locked under her power. Andrea felt omnipotent. She decided to pull him to bed for one more month before signing the agreement.

For Udit, he was about to reach the breaking point. He knew that with the signing of the agreement he would have sold his soul to Andrea. She would eat his body alive. One evening after a tumultuous sex, Andrea said, "Now we are ready for the agreement signing function my dear Udit. After that I'll take you to my beachside villa..."

Udit had to wear a mask and also act out his enjoyment, by forgetting that he was cheating his loving wife for a good future, when he and the others celebrated Jaseela's birthday. The disgust that Udit felt while making love to Jaseela had to be hidden from her as well lest she figure out. The next day Jaseela had a class to take in the same school where the children were studying. After Jaseela and the children left, Udit sat at the dining table and cried his heart out. The immense emotional trauma that he was going through... Would he end up like Jonathan or Heyson? All of a sudden Udit felt scared to sit alone in that flat. He wanted his family badly. He didn't pick the incessant calls of Andrea. Udit ignored Andrea's calls for two days. Five more days were left for the agreement to be signed for his project to start rolling. On the third day, Udit mustered enough strength to sabotage his new-found future. He called Andrea and told her he was withdrawing from the project. Andrea knew that, she said. She also mentioned in a passive manner that Udit would never make a film ever again. She would do the needful. Andrea cut the call.

CHAPTER XXXI

Mohith

"You are the father", said Kannaki with blood-shot eyes, with anger dancing like a raging fire. She spoke these words to Mohith, the six-pack hunky celebrity star. All the enthusiasm of having done his part perfectly well in the trial take of the single shot and the following enjoyment with the cast and crew in the royal hall singing 'Happy Birthday' to Bhagath, had all but faded into the distance. Before Kannaki took Srividya away secretly to the border hospital that evening, she did find time to trace out Mohith. She knew where he would be. He was having a good sleep after a wild time with a junior artist; he had promised her a good role in his upcoming debut feature film. Kannaki had her mind hell bent on tearing Mohith apart ever since she got ousted from the project, ever since that rough sex session. She wanted to win.

Kannaki was sure Mohith would sink, sink miserably. And that was what exactly happened. Kannaki saw the opportune moment was now. She simply told a lie. She had no second thoughts about that act. She had one objective. She took the chance. And boy was it a sight to see Mohith simply stand there seeping in that shocking information. Mohith had a great muscular body. He pumped up the muscles when he got the role of the menacing army general. And with fame, money and women all around him, Mohith felt he was infallible. He thought he was a rough and tough dude. Mohith even devised a signature move that he had planned to endorse in all the public functions he would appear. His move would become legendary in the industry in the coming years.

Mohith fell to the floor with a thud and cried unabashedly. Kannaki was right. All those assumptions Mohith built up were just balloons tied up together. She had just to poke those balloons with a pin. And there came down Mohith crashing and shattering. Kannaki also knew Mohith wouldn't go seeking Srividya. He didn't have the guts to do that. Kannaki despised men for their made-up guts. She hated everybody. She hated herself. Kannaki left the room leaving Mohith to writhe in pain. Mohith had destroyed the life of a young woman. He did make love to Srividya a couple of weeks back. He may have given her a child. He didn't know... All the roughness and toughness simply melted away. Having learnt that Srividya was not there in the set, Mohith left the place. He told no one. He wanted to see no one.

Srividya was thinking about Heyson as she sipped a cold pineapple juice and ate the chicken biriyani aboard the chartered flight to the UK. She had a funeral to attend, and she was also planning to meet Wendy. Srividya had a great urge to go attend Heyson's funeral back then. But Kannaki wouldn't allow that. The storm had to die down. Srividya had a stupendous career to build. That was to be her only priority. And through those five years, Srividya had only thought of her career. All those five years. Not once did she visit Jaseela or Anju or Smitha. Anju Leelavathi. A sister from another mother. Srividya ached within. She hated this acting business. Srividya wanted to stop acting and do something else. Maybe take tuition for children. She loved children. Ever since she had to give up her first child, the mother in Srividya hadn't departed. Srividya knew she wouldn't marry or settle down in this current life. Superstar Srividya had seen enough. Without Kannaki noticing,

Srividya wiped away a few tears that had gathered in her eyes preparing to roll down her cheeks. One cloud in the distance resembled a baby's tiny head. Srividya touched the cold window and stared at that cloud.

Kannaki saw Srividya wiping her tears away. She was filled with her own thoughts. Mohith. Five years down the line, Kannaki felt what she did had exceeded the limit. She shouldn't have taken revenge in that manner. Kannaki had grown older. She was more mature now. She was quieter now. She had begun to lose all the grand ambitions that once drove her forward. Now, she was a slave. Srividya's slave. And yet she endured. This was her doing. And she had to toil. A sort of repentance. The only window of happiness that came her way was the occasional video calls with Jasmine, Jaseela or the other women. They were in different places, but rowing the same boat.

After the return from the UK Kannaki had planned to take a few months off and fly down to Kolaazham and visit her girls. Her boys too. She wanted to pay a visit to Venkatesh's house. They had become pals just before Venkatesh went. Kannaki also wanted to go and see Mohith. She knew where he had escaped to. Mohith did his debut feature film and then left the industry for good. He was now in the outskirts of Nepal, running a bike repair shop. There he assumed a different name. So said one of the innumerable connections Kannaki had, who tracked down Mohith. The very thought of getting to meet the man severely destroyed by her brought painful tears to Kannaki's eyes. She rushed to the toilet.

CHAPTER XXXII

Bleak

The newspapers and television channels were filled with tributes to one of the wealthiest and visionary producers the West had ever produced. And what was what people called a divine intervention was the day in particular in which Jonathan Meg died. Jonathan's derangement fell into a severe condition in the initial years. But from the fourth year of confinement and treatment Jonathan had begun to show signs of improvement. He could recognise Elsa and his three children. Memories returned when Tim stood in front of him, with Wendy. Wendy was pregnant again. The memories that came back were harsh ones, not the kind the backstabber Tim would expect. Jonathan got angry for the first time with his senses back. That was a giant leap as regards progress.

Elsa thanked Tim for presenting himself with his wife to Jonathan. But later she would regret that act. Because Jonathan had called in Elsa and requested her to help him with his will. As expected, most of her parents' property and money went back to Elsa. But Jonathan made her write a clause which stipulated that the withheld remunerations of every member of The Rhino Emperor be given out, with an additional Rs 25 lakhs each for the delay caused by his production company. He also sought forgiveness from the entire team of the series. Elsa was angry at Jonathan for that one point.

Once the will was drawn out and made legal, Jonathan spoke no more and neither did he wish to see anyone, not even his children. Jonathan realised one thing now; he had flown to London before the trial shoot of the long duration single shot five years ago. Somewhere within Jonathan there was a constant yearning to return to that surreal film set. Kumar and his team had done a wonderful job. Jonathan had such good times in The Rhino Emperor's set during the first season's entire production. He missed those days. He missed Kolaazham. He missed Jaseela a lot. What was she doing now? Why did he allow his mind to wander off under that shower, with ludicrous thoughts and finally destroy so many lives including his? Jonathan dreamt of a serene day in the set. There was only Jaseela and himself now. They ran about like children. They enjoyed the apples and mangoes kept in the shops built into the set. They bathed in the lake. And then Jonathan held Jaseela in his arms. Jonathan smiled... He passed away on the exact day the production of The Rhino Emperor came to a grinding halt.

The news of the demise had reached the entire team of the erstwhile series. Srividya took a chartered flight to London to be there for the funeral. She also had plans to meet Wendy. She wanted to foray into British television. This was the opportune moment to talk to Wendy. Kannaki tagged along. She had to. At the airport Kannaki tried to contact Jaseela and Udit. They didn't take the calls. She informed the others. She asked Jasmine, who lived near Jaseela's flat, to go to her and inform about the remuneration part. Jasmine first ran out of her clinic in the middle of checking a patient. She ran into her pharmacist husband and asked him to come to the stock room. A confused Thomas marched into the stock room. Jasmine kissed her husband immediately. A surprised Thomas just stood there seeping in the moment. Once the kiss was done, Jasmine conveyed the information. Thomas stood with dazed eyes. Laughing at Thomas' expression Jasmine ran out, with Jaseela's flat in mind.

Jaseela was in for a shock. No not because of Jonathan's death. She thought she had seen a glimmer of hope when Udit told her about Andromeda films. Her heart was breaking. She couldn't breathe. Her tears rolled over her cheeks and fell onto the hair of Udit who was lying on her lap with his face dipped in his own tears. Udit could take it no longer. He waited for Jaseela and the children to return. He broke down hitting his head with his hands and calling himself a whore for selling his body to start a film project. Jaseela loved Udit. She loved the vulnerable man in Udit. Of late Udit had rebuilt that impregnable fortress and guarded his flailing feelings as regards their lives. Jaseela understood the situation really well. She knew the circumstances under which Udit caved. Jaseela couldn't desert her husband now or forever. She caressed Udit with all her love. She saw the desperation behind that illicit act. She placed him on her lap and caressed his hair. Slowly, slowly Udit stopped crying. He felt the pain and disgust of that dishonest affair wash away slowly. He lay on Jaseela's lap and stayed there, in that warmth. Udit felt a strong sense of protection.

All this time both Jaseela's and Udit's phones were ringing. But the deeply troubled couple didn't hear the ringtones. They both saw a deep void in front of them. Emptiness. Jaseela asked herself if she would end up like Heyson? Or would she lose her sanity like Jonathan?... Why was she thinking about Jonathan now? On the day Jonathan died, that day, Jaseela did feel something, a telepathic shockwave reverberate across her body. She saw Jonathan... She held onto Udit tightly. She told about that experience to Udit. Udit hugged her. When their children came to them, the four-member family sat there on the floor with hopeful smiles on their faces but with empty hearts. Yet they wished for something good that would finally come to them. And like in a slow transition where one scene overlaps onto the other in films, Udit's and Jaseela's minds slipped to the last day they spent on The Rhino Emperor's set.

Jaseela stood near the dismantled arena close to the lake, which was supposed to be the location for the duel between Margafa and Himsha to take place in S02E03. Her hands were held tightly between Udit's as she visualised that epic sword fight. Jaseela also had a gigantic sea battle in mind, to be placed somewhere in the third season. Those scenes were playing on Jaseela's mind's screen. Udit and Jaseela kept staring at the distance. The gentle waves from the man-made lake were reflecting the setting sun's rays onto the couple's faces. Now, Jaseela wrapped herself so close to Udit she could hear his heartbeat clearly. She wanted his warmth. Her mind felt at peace even though she had lost her greatest dream. Jaseela heaved a slight sigh. Udit knew what the woman of his future life was ruminating about. She was thinking about the goosebumps that that surreal single shot would have given to her, to the whole team, had it materialised. That long duration single shot... Now, Jaseela was keen on forgetting that dream. Once they walked out of the compound, that dream would perish. Jaseela lost in that endeavour. Udit stood with the loser. He loved Jaseela. He looked at Jaseela. She looked at Udit. There, there stood the real naked selves of both of them. Two vulnerable humans. Two simple humans. They kissed under that sudden realisation, beside the heavenly twilight, and then watched the sun slowly descend behind the Western Ghats leaving the lake a tad dark. They then turned towards the other side and sat there on the dusty ground with watery eyes, watching Production Designer Kumar and his team slowly dismantle the remaining sets of the monumental television series The Rhino Emperor.

Also By The Author

1. Life and Times in Kolaazham Part 1 (a collection of forty short stories)

2. Koodumbol Imbam (a spec screenplay in Manglish)

3. There Came Down A Nightingale and other poems (a collection of twenty one poems)

4. Nalanda (a spec screenplay in Manglish)

5. Elegy (a spec screenplay in Malayalam)

6. Life and Times in Kolaazham Part II: Founder's Day (a collection of one hundred eleven short stories)

These books are available on the Notion Press website, Amazon and Flipkart. Do buy these books, read and share your reviews on Amazon and Flipkart.

You can share your feedback at devji4@gmail.com